Diverse Lives

Diverse Lives
Contemporary Stories from Indonesia

Translated and Introduced by
JEANETTE LINGARD

KUALA LUMPUR
OXFORD UNIVERSITY PRESS
OXFORD SINGAPORE NEW YORK
1995

Oxford University Press

Oxford New York
Athens Auckland Bangkok Bombay
Calcutta Cape Town Dar es Salaam Delhi
Florence Hong Kong Istanbul Karachi
Madras Madrid Melbourne Mexico City
Nairobi Paris Shah Alam Singapore
Taipei Tokyo Toronto

and associated companies in
Berlin Ibadan

Oxford is a trade mark of Oxford University Press

Published in the United States
by Oxford University Press, New York

British Library Cataloguing in Publication Data
Data available

Library of Congress Cataloging-in-Publication Data
Diverse lives: contemporary stories from Indonesia/translated and
introduced by Jeanette Lingard.
p. cm. — (Oxford in Asia paperbacks)
Translated from Indonesian.
ISBN 967 65 3100 6 (pbk.)
1. Short stories, Indonesian—Translations into English.
2. Indonesian fiction—20th century—Translations into English.
I. Lingard, Jeanette. II. Series.
PL5088.2.E5D59   1995
899'.22130108—dc20
95-35645
CIP

Typeset by EXPO Holdings, Malaysia
Printed by KHL Printing Co. Pte. Ltd., Singapore
Published by the South-East Asian Publishing Unit,
a division of Penerbit Fajar Bakti Sdn. Bhd.,
under licence from Oxford University Press,
4 Jalan U1/15, Seksyen U1, 40000 Shah Alam,
Selangor Darul Ehsan, Malaysia

Contents

Introduction

JEANETTE LINGARD

SINCE the 1940s the short story has established itself as a very popular literary form in modern Indonesian literature. Indeed, the critic Supardi Djoko Damano comments, 'The short story is inseparable from our daily lives.' Perhaps the reason that the short story finds fertile ground is because of the long tradition of story-telling which exists in Indonesia, an oral tradition that is now being expressed in a written form.

Perhaps too there is a pragmatic reason for the growth of interest in writing short stories. The monetary returns from writing are not great, but the strong demand for stories from the popular press provides a financial incentive for writers. In the cities, short stories proliferate in popular magazines, newspapers—particularly on Sundays—and in the literary magazine *Horison*. Each year the leading Jakarta newspaper *Kompas* publishes an anthology of its best short stories for that particular year. Periodically, short story competitions are also held. The brevity of many short stories is also explained by the fact that they are written for the limited space available in the newspapers and magazines. Compared with the number of novels published, the number of anthologies of short stories is quite small.

Many of the stories written between the 1950s and 1970s have portrayed the great upheavals in Indonesian society of the time—the Japanese occupation, the proclamation of independence, the revolution against the Dutch and its aftermath, internal rebellions, the abortive coup of 1965, and the bloodbath which followed it, the demise of Soekarno's Old Order regime, and the emergence of the New Order Government under President Soeharto. This period has been represented in previous collections of stories translated into English.

When I began to contemplate this collection of contemporary Indonesian short stories, I decided to concentrate on stories written in the 1980s and early 1990s, a time of consolidation of the New Order, bringing with it political stability, development, economic growth, and increasing contact with the West. Fewer of the stories written in this period have been published in English, compared with the earlier period mentioned above. I wanted to find stories which would perhaps show something of the lives of people in this New Order society; people living in cities, kampongs— which may be town quarters or urban slums—and rural villages, people from the emerging, wealthy, middle class, and people from the poor echelons of society.

Having established the time frame, my aim was to make this as representative a collection as possible and try to include the work of writers from different parts of the archipelago, men and women. In a sense I have been able to achieve the first part of this aim as a number of authors were actually born outside Java, although the vast majority of them now live and work in Java. I have not achieved the second part of my aim, as ten of the thirteen authors represented here are men. Regarding the dearth of women writers, Keith Foulcher points out that 'Indonesian fiction in the New Order period, like modern Indonesian literature throughout its history, has largely been an art form practised by men. Women poets and writers have been the exceptions to a norm, always marked in Indonesian terminology as "penulis wanita", woman writer, and "penyair wanita", woman poet, which practice seems to suggest that the Indonesian terms for "writer" and "poet" indicate the male gender.' However, I have managed to find two fine stories by women—one, 'The Chickens', by Indonesia's best-known woman writer, N. H. Dini, and the other, 'Sita's Holy Water', by the young writer, Leila Chudori.

Some of the stories are by long-established writers such as Putu Wijaya, Budi Darma, N. H. Dini, and Satyagraha Hoerip, but most are by a younger generation of writers who are making their mark on the Indonesian literary scene. It was another aim of my selection to identify and introduce the work of some of these young writers. As can be seen in the biographical notes which accompany each of the stories, the authors are very versatile, writing creatively in a number of genres.

There is, of course, an element of chance in the selection of stories for translation and inclusion in an anthology such as this. Much depends on the availability of stories, and I acknowledge that there must be many stories worthy of inclusion in a collection of contemporary stories—by writers Javanese and non-Javanese, men and women—which I have not had the opportunity to find in the time available to me.

There is no single thematic basis for my collection. The choice is purely a reflection of my personal taste, stories I read and liked, which I feel have literary merit, and which tell the reader something of the life experiences and concerns of a range of characters in contemporary Indonesian society. Most of the stories are characterized by realism, with some forays into fantasy, and most are generated by conflict, literal or figurative. This may be the conflict within an individual, conflict between individuals, or conflict between individuals and society.

Whether these stories are tragic, ironic, fantastic, shocking, amusing, or poignant, my hope is that they will appeal to the general reader.

Among the many challenges facing a translator is that of translating 'cultural' words and concepts from the source language when there is no equivalent in the target language. Many of these words pertain to material culture, such as food, clothing, and housing. For example, when Indonesian women attend special or official functions they wear a set of traditional clothes called *kain kebaya*. In 'The Corpse' and 'The Special Gift', these clothes are mentioned, and I have chosen to use English glosses for these terms rather than break the flow of the story with a footnote. I have used this technique wherever possible. However, in some instances when the name of a culture-specific food or plant is mentioned, I have retained the original form as the context is enough to show in general terms what is being referred to.

A variation of the problem occurs when a common word such as *rumah* which means 'house' or 'home' is used in 'The Palace Walls'. The word 'house' evokes an image of a Western house, which is quite inappropriate in the Balinese context, and I have avoided using the word. It is necessary to know that a traditional Balinese 'house' takes the form of a walled compound in which are a number of detached pavilion-like buildings, each of which is used for a separate function, such as sleeping, cooking, eating, and the conduct of ceremonies.

Terms of reference or address provide another problem. In Indonesian and in Javanese, which is sometimes used in some of these stories, kinship terms such as 'mother', 'father', 'uncle', 'aunty', 'brother', and 'sister' can be used to refer to or address people who are not relatives, to show either respect or intimacy. For example, in two of these stories, 'The Men Who Laughed' and 'The Madman', the Javanese word 'Lik' is used in this way for two peripheral characters. I have used the word 'uncle' for these characters, who may or may not have been real uncles in these instances.

Similarly, the words 'Bapak' and its short form 'Pak', and 'Ibu' or 'Bu', which mean respectively 'father' and 'mother', are used either alone or before given or family names to show respect. When used alone to address someone, the nearest English equivalent would be the formal 'Sir' or 'Madam', which is not always appropriate for the Indonesian context. In such cases, I have used the more natural English 'you'. When used before a name, 'Pak' and 'Bu' can be the equivalent of 'Mr' and 'Mrs'. However, I have chosen to retain the Indonesian terms for the characters 'Bu Kustiyah' and 'Pak Hargi' in 'The Special Gift' with the hope that 'Pak' and 'Bu' will become as familiar to English readers as 'Monsieur', 'Madame', 'Herr', 'Frau', 'Signore', and 'Signora' are when they are used for 'foreign' characters in English stories, without being translated as 'Mr' and 'Mrs'.

Finally, I wish to express my thanks to Nyoman Darma Putra, for his suggestions about stories and particularly for bringing to my attention the work of the Balinese writer Gde Aryantha Soethama; to Nuraini Ali, for clarification of some of the cultural aspects; to Lea Brown for her perceptive and helpful comments; and finally to the writers themselves, for their stories and for allowing me to use them in this collection.

References

Supardi Djoko Damano, *Kesusasteraan Indonesia Modern*, Jakarta: PT Gramedia, 1983.

Foulcher, K., 'Some Trends in Indonesian Fiction', in Virginia Matheson Hooker (ed.), *Culture and Society in New Order Indonesia*, Kuala Lumpur: Oxford University Press, 1993.

The Special Gift

JUJUR PRANANTO

Jujur Prananto was born in Salatiga, Java, in 1960, did his schooling in Yogyakarta and now lives in Jakarta, where he studied cinematography at the Jakarta Arts Institute. He has worked as an assistant film director and has worked on screen plays. He has been writing since his high school days, and his short stories have been published in several Jakarta newspapers. This story, 'The Special Gift', was first published in *Kompas* in 1992. It was then selected for inclusion in an anthology, called *The Special Gift*, of the best fifteen stories published by *Kompas* in 1992. The selection panel named this story as the best of the fifteen.

The story tells of a woman who journeys from her home in a small town in Central Java to Jakarta to see, for the first time in many years, her former commander in the time of the guerrilla war against the Dutch, now a high official in the New Order regime. Time has wrought many changes.

BU KUSTIYAH was absolutely determined to attend the wedding reception for Pak Hargi's son. She had to, no matter what the difficulties and no matter what it cost. She'd made up her mind long ago that when the time came for Pak Hargi to marry off his children, she would go and congratulate him, say how thrilled she was and show that she still respected him, even though times had changed.

'Pak Hargi was my senior officer and I really respected him,' Bu Kustiyah often told her neighbours. 'He was a true freedom fighter, one of those who fought to establish this country. Even though I only worked in the camp cook-house, I felt happy and proud to serve with him.'

However, according to Bu Kustiyah, after the capital was moved back to Jakarta from Yogyakarta, things changed a lot. Pak Hargi was assigned to Jakarta and she only occasionally heard news of him. Time passed with no contact between them. Trouble was looming, and after the abortive coup in September 1965, the distance between Kalasan and Jakarta seemed even greater. Then the collapse of the Old Order regime and the emergence of Soeharto's New Order strengthened Pak Hargi's role in the central government. This meant there was even less likelihood of any direct communication between him and Bu Kustiyah. But it didn't mean that she felt distant from him because, as she said herself, sharing the same ideals was an unbreakable bond between them.

'In the old days we often used to talk about these ideals with the other guerrilla fighters,' she reminisced. 'At such times, whenever any of the others dreamed how wonderful it would be when victory was won, Pak Gi often stressed that the struggle against poverty and ignorance was just as important as the struggle against the return of the Dutch.'

But even though Bu Kus always felt close to Pak Gi, apparently after no contact for over thirty years, she had a great longing to see him in person and talk about old times. When she heard the news that he was marrying off his son, she made up her mind that this would be the ideal opportunity to see him.

*   *   *

It was past midday. Bu Kustiyah had finished her lunch and couldn't bear staying in the house a minute longer. She picked up her leather suitcase that had been packed since the previous day, and also a big plastic bag full of all sorts of presents for her grandchildren in Jakarta. Feeling that all the odds and ends had been taken care of, she told the woman who helped her in the house to call a horse cart to take her to the railway station.

Before three o'clock she was already sitting on the platform even though the economy class train to Jakarta didn't leave till six. Her rush to get away from the house had made her even more impatient. She felt she wanted to get to Jakarta as soon as possible to greet Pak Hargi and talk about the old days with him: about sweet memories of the cookhouse, the rice that had to be served up half-cooked, the courier Ngatimin, who was so clever at hiding, and Nyai Kemuning, a female occupant of the barracks who filled the dreams of the young men. Ah, there were so many amusing stories that she felt could never be forgotten despite the effects of the turning of the wheel of time.

The train whistle startled Bu Kus. She stood up quickly and hurried to get into the carriage.

'Hold it, lady, the train's just being shunted.'

But Bu Kus's feet were already firmly planted on the steps of the carriage.

'Just as long as it gets to Jakarta.'

'We haven't allocated the seat numbers yet.'

'I've got my ticket and that's all I care about.'

*   *   *

So, after going through such long-drawn-out anxiety, at last
Bu Kus arrived in Jakarta. Wawuk, her daughter, nearly
died of shock when her mother turned up on the doorstep
early in the morning after getting out of a taxi all by herself.

'There's no doubt about you, mother. Why didn't you
tell us you were coming?'

'I sent you a telegram, didn't I?'

'Yes, but you didn't say exactly when you were coming.'

'The important thing is that I'm here.'

'That's fine, but if we'd known when you were coming,
we'd have picked you up at the station.'

'I didn't want to put you to any trouble. And anyway, I
left in a rush, because I was frightened I might miss the
wedding reception for Pak Gi's son and daughter-in-law.
It's your fault, too. You didn't mention the exact date of it
in your letter.'

'Oh my God! Are you going to the reception?'

'You're the one who told me Pak Gi's son was getting
married.'

'Why didn't you write and tell me you were doing that?'

'Do I have to tell you every little detail?'

'Of course you don't.' Wawuk wasn't sure how to go on.
'Mother, you haven't been invited, have you?'

'You don't think they'll turn me away if I haven't got an
invitation, do you?'

'No, of course not. But they'll probably have seats for the
VIPs and ordinary seats and you won't know which are
which.'

'Come on now, it's a wedding. They're not going to
have VIP seats like they do at the *wayang* dance dramas.'

'There's another thing, mother, I have no idea where the
reception will be held or when or what time. I only know

about the wedding from Totok and he's only heard from gossip around the place.'

'Your husband works in the same office as Pak Gi, doesn't he? Do you expect me to believe he wasn't invited?'

'Not in the same office, the same department. Besides, Totok is just an ordinary official, far lower down the scale than Pak Gi. And not even directly under him, so he knows absolutely nothing about all this, let alone the issuing of invitations.'

'He could ask, couldn't he?'

Wawuk heaved a loud sigh.

'Now you listen to me, Wuk,' Bu Kus said in a low voice, 'I've come all this way to Jakarta for one thing, and one thing only, and that is to go to the wedding reception for Pak Hargi's son.'

*   *   *

Getting information about where and when the reception would be held turned out to be no problem at all for Wawuk's husband. Pak Hargi was a top-level official in a very important position. So important was his job that metaphorically speaking, if he suffered flu symptoms, even just the symptoms, it seemed the whole department would find out about it. That's why it was easy for Wawuk's husband to get all the details, including a copy of the invitation to the reception.

'It's at seven o'clock tomorrow night in the Puri Agung room at the Sahid Jaya Hotel.'

'God help us! At a hotel?'

'Yes, mother.'

'Not in an ordinary building?'

'At hotels they have special rooms for receptions.'

'Ohhh....'

'Well, I suppose they do. I've never really been inside one.'

'But you do know where the hotel is, don't you, Totok?'

'Yes, I know, mother.'

*   *   *

In the middle of the night, it was Wawuk's turn to be unable to sleep. Her mind was in turmoil with all sorts of confused feelings. She desperately wanted to stop her mother from going to the reception, but she really had no reason to do so. She couldn't possibly say, 'Why do you have to go to a reception given by someone who'll surely have forgotten you?' or 'After all, they won't be expecting us,' or some other excuse which, instead of dissuading her mother, would quite likely make her even more determined to go just so she could say, 'I told you so, Wuk.'

On the other hand, Wawuk also felt guilty. Why, deep down, did she feel ashamed of her own mother? Wherever did such wicked feelings come from when she really did have the greatest respect for her? She respected her simplicity, her idealism, and her moral attitudes. Why was her respect for those values so easily shaken just because her mother was going to attend a party at a five-star hotel?

Wawuk got up out of bed, and went quietly to her mother's room. It was empty. Her gaze fell on her mother's leather case on the bed. She opened it and recognized the traditional batik sarong and formal blouse inside the case as ones her mother had owned for the past five or six years. Wawuk remembered once when she'd wanted to buy her mother some clothes that were a bit better and her mother had refused for some reason or other. Those black slippers too, goodness knows how many times the soles had been mended.

Suddenly, Wawuk heard the sound of a pan falling and she hurried to the kitchen. She felt even more confused when she saw her mother busy cooking. On the table was a woven bamboo tray that had been lined with a white embroidered cloth. Some small baskets were arranged neatly on it. On the stove sat a large pot sending up thick clouds of steam.

'What's that you're cooking, mother?'

Cassava snacks.'

Cassava snacks? Whatever for?'

'I spent days looking for a present that would be just right for Pak Hargi's son. Something unique, special, and most importantly, something meaningful. It wasn't till yesterday that I hit on the right choice. Why not the food we ate during the days of the revolution? Later, when he sees a present that's so different from the others, Pak Gi's son will be certain to ask his father about it. I'm sure Pak Gi will be very impressed and he'll explain all about the significance of this food in the days of the revolution. At the very least, his son will get a picture of the reality of the past that his father experienced. Ah yes, this gift will certainly be the most important of all. Special and at the same time significant.'

'But they might go bad, mightn't they?'

'If I make them, they'll last up to three days.'

Wawuk stood like a statue. She was lost for words.

*   *   *

Tight security covered the reception room of the Sahid Jaya Hotel. In the grounds, security men, complete with black suits and walkie-talkies, swarmed everywhere. The entry door was only half open, a metre or so wide, and was fitted with a metal detector alarm.

Bu Kus looked at it all in amazement. She tightly clutched the brown-paper wrapped gift box that she'd had prepared for so long. The guests were entering the reception room couple by couple, each carrying the twenty by twenty-five centimetre gold-engraved invitation. Putting on a false show of bravado, Totok and Wuwuk joined the stream of guests, escorting Bu Kus, who preceded them through the door.

'Good evening, madam.'

'Good evening, good evening.'

Bu Kus handed over her present to one of the pretty attendants receiving the guests.

'Please store this gift of mine carefully, miss. Make sure you put it the right way up or it will all spill. It contains very special food.'

'Thank you, madam. Please go on in. But would you mind not going up to the bridal party's dais before the President's entourage arrives.'

'Good heavens, do you mean to say the President is coming too?'

Bu Kus was even more excited when she went into the reception room. Much clicking of her tongue accompanied her amazement at this most beautiful, large, and luxurious room. In various places around the room were long tables holding food and drinks, and decorated with arrangements of coloured candles and giant ice sculptures. And on the far side of the room, on a raised, golden coloured dais, sat the bridal couple and their respective parents. Leading to the dais was a red carpet strewn with jasmine flowers, and to the right and left of this stood a line of young men and women, a fine and beautiful cordon, all dressed in yellow silk outfits with swathes of dark red lace.

But Bu Kus couldn't relax until she met Pak Gi, and for that to happen a great deal of patience was still needed. All the guests had to wait over half an hour until the President's party arrived. As soon as they came, exchanged greetings, had some photos taken with the bridal party, and departed, about two

thousand guests jostled to get in the queue leading to the dais.
In place number one thousand and something or other was
Bu Kus trying hard to stand still, with her feelings in turmoil.

After about an hour of being crowded and jostled, she
reached the dais. She was overcome with emotion and in
her heart whispered her thanks to Almighty God.

With trembling hands, she greeted Pak Gi.

'You haven't changed a bit, Pak Gi. You still look so
young. Congratulations.'

'Thank you, thank you.'

Bu Kus couldn't contain herself and she lunged at his
hand, kissing it and sobbing.

'It's Kustiyah. It's me, Kustiyah. From the cookhouse.'

Pak Gi frowned but then quickly regained his compos-
ure, giving the impression he was used to dealing with situ-
ations of this kind.

'Oh yes, yes of course it is. Thank you.'

'The Kalasan post, sir. There was Aris, and Dal, and
Ngatimin the dwarf. Now they're all in Semarang.'

'Oh yes, yes.'

'They're all there, still all together. But don't ask me
about Nyai Kemuning,' she laughed through her tears.

'Yes. I see. Thank you so much. Thank you.'

'When can we get together for a good chat, Pak Gi?'

For a moment, he was lost for words. His wife was a
little tense. The guests were starting to mutter because the
queue was held up.

'Umm…. Any time. Thank you for coming.'

'It's my pleasure. Once again, congratulations.'

'Yes, yes, thank you.'

'Well, so this is your son, is it? Why, he's the image of
you when you were young.'

After she'd greeted everyone, Bu Kus finally left the dais.
The queue started moving again after the brief hold-up.

Everyone was relieved. But no one's relief could equal hers. She felt that the incredibly beautiful and huge reception room warmly welcomed her presence. She invited Totok and Wawuk to explore the whole room, and taste all the various kinds of food.

'Pak Gi really is a fighter who has never forgotten his ideals.'

'Which ideals would they be, mother?'

'That just as important as the struggle against the Dutch was the one against poverty and ignorance. Isn't all this proof of his success in that struggle?'

'Why didn't you ever follow in his footsteps, mother?'

'As a former member of the cookhouse division, I *am* still carrying on the struggle! Against hunger....'

*   *   *

It was a week later, at the bridal couple's house, in the room where the wedding gifts were stored. The bridegroom sprawled wearily with his legs stretched out on the sofa while his brand new wife was busy making an inventory of the gifts, including those still stored in plastic bags that hadn't been opened since the reception.

'Hallo, newlyweds!'

A crowd of family members had arrived. The groom got to his feet and the bride looked relieved.

'So what's taken you so long to get here? I've got a headache from sorting out all these presents. Anyway, just pick out something that you'd like. What we got most of were clocks, and there are sixteen irons, twenty-five sets of sheets, and five refrigerators, but we're keeping two of those for ourselves and the others are all taken. There are lots of those lovely teasets plus table lamps, wall lamps, thermos flasks, towels, condoms. Just help yourselves, take anything you want.'

'Did you get any car keys?'

'Would you believe a BMW?'

'Wow—cool! What about the keys of a house?'

'Of course we did.'

'Money? Did you get some of those envelopes with money in them?'

'They're already in the bank.'

'What's in this bag here?'

'Tip it out, empty it!'

'Shit! It stinks!'

All attention was focused on a gift wrapped in brown paper. It looked soggy in the corners. When it was opened, they didn't know the name of the food in the woven bamboo tray covered with the white embroidered cloth. It had spilled everywhere and had gone mouldy in places. There was a piece of paper with writing on it that was hard to read because the red palm sugar had melted and made the ink run.

'Bu Kus, Kustijak … Kustiah. Who on earth is she?'

The bridegroom inspected the gift. 'How the hell would I know? Imah!'

A woman servant appeared.

'Get that stuff out of here!'

'Where do you want me to put it, sir?'

'Put it? Throw it out!'

The Palace Walls

GDE ARYANTHA SOETHAMA

Gde Aryantha Soethama was born in Bali in 1955, and still lives and works there. After completing tertiary studies in agriculture, he turned to journalism. Between 1981 and 1990, he held editorial positions on newspapers, and has written and published three books on journalism. His poetry and short stories have been published in various newspapers, and two anthologies of his short stories were published in 1984 and 1985 respectively. In addition, he has published two plays, and one of his novels has won first place in a literary competition.

In his two stories in this collection, Gde Aryantha Soethama takes the reader to a Bali that the tourist does not see or influence in any way, a place where tradition holds firm. 'The Palace Walls' was published in *Kompas* in 1993. In it the author tells a touching story of the dilemma faced by a young woman who marries above her station, in the hierarchical Balinese social structure.

MANY of the girls were envious when Kadek Sumerti received a marriage proposal from the family of Anak Agung Ngurah Parwata. For them, the nobility epitomized the pinnacle of respect, power, and forgiving tolerance when they did wrong.

'It'll be wonderful for her living in the palace, with lots of space and high walls around her,' the girls chattered.

'Her name will be longer. She'll have the title commoners get when they marry into the nobility. She'll be called Jero Kadek Sumerti.'

'When there's a traditional function, she'll be sitting up in the place of honour. We'll be on the floor and she'll be up on the special dais.'

'Of course, she'll be in a different social class from us.'

'It must be her destiny to be born a commoner and marry into the nobility.'

Of course, none of the girls knew about the mental struggle Kadek had to go through before she decided to become one of the nobility. Only her great and true love for Anak Agung Ngurah enabled her to solve the dilemma. Ngurah also kept coaxing her and telling her it wasn't difficult being a member of the nobility nowadays.

'Our home might be a palace, but the people in it are modern,' Ngurah said. 'You'll see for yourself, we have a refrigerator, a laser disc, a parabola antenna and all sorts of trappings of modern life. There's no reason why you shouldn't be able to adapt.'

'There'll still be a lot of other problems for me when I talk to the family in the palace.'

'For example?'

'For example, I'll have to use high Balinese with them all the time.'

Anak Agung Ngurah Parwata smiled. 'You've already seen for youself every time I've invited you to the palace that you can use Indonesian. They accept you gladly, no matter what. They know we're modern people and so are they.'

'Maybe the younger ones are, but what about the elders?'

'These days they're modern too. When we speak to them, we don't have to prostrate ourselves any more.

They're used to using the telephone to let other members of the family know if there's a traditional ceremony in the palace. They watch American serials on television. Several of them speak Indonesian when they receive guests and no longer use high Balinese. They're just like us. You know how modernization gets people in, including the older generation. They can't resist it either, Ti!'

Kadek Sumerti was confused. She really did doubt whether she could become one of the nobility, living on land with high walls around it among people who always considered the weakening of traditional values as tantamount to the collapse of self-respect.

'You must become my wife, Ti. We've already agreed.'

'But I can't help doubting whether I'll be able to cope with being in the nobility. I've had no experience of living in a large family with strict rules.'

'The palace rules nowadays accommodate modern people like us. Everything will fall into place in due course. Trust me. However long it takes, you must accept. If you don't, we'll never see each other again.'

*   *   *

Finally, they did get married. Kadek Sumerti was very uneasy when the noble family arranged the wedding with full pomp and ceremony. Her parents were amazed, never thinking for one minute that such glorious honour would be bestowed on their house.

'Really, this sort of thing is not necessary, Par. My family doesn't want any fuss. We just don't know what to do.'

'This isn't much, Ti. It's simpler than the usual way we do things. The palace wants to honour your family because they've willingly allowed one of their daughters to enter our circle for love, not because they've been coerced into it as used to happen with our family in the past. You are mine because you want to be, not as booty. This is a modern marriage even if it's still got the flavour of the palace about it.'

Everyday life in the palace these days really was modern. Before their marriage, there were nineteen families living there. Anak Agung Ngurah Parwata and Kadek Sumerti became the twentieth. All the families had their own quarters, and didn't feel that they bothered each other, even though four generations were living there.

Kadek was free to visit her family whenever she wanted to. When she talked to people in the palace, she used the same manners as she did with her friends or parents. The palace gates were never locked and she was free to come and go as she pleased.

'I told you the palace is modern now, didn't I?' Ngurah said one time.

'Yes, but people still think that inside these walls weird etiquette and customs are always observed.'

'What's weird? If things are so weird, how could I possibly have married you? In the old days it really was weird, when people had to offer their virgin daughters to the palace. You've proved things have changed. We approached you for this marriage, because we respect the nature of the family that raised you.'

Kadek Sumerti's family certainly were accorded more respect since one of their daughters entered the palace nobility with the right to use the title 'Jero'. When people talked about the Sumerti family, they'd whisper, 'Oh are they the ones whose daughter married into the palace?'

*   *   *

But the palace was still the palace. It still had solid walls around it, the legacy of past centuries. The gates might be open all the time but the walls were not allowed to collapse. In those walls, the awesomeness of the palace resided, guarded for generations by their authenticity. The walls ensured the sanctity of the palace so that it endured as the focal point of the community. Kadek Sumerti experienced this when she'd been married for almost a year.

Her family was arranging a traditional tooth-filing ceremony especially for Kadek and her brothers and sister. This ceremony was always the responsibility of parents to their children and was normally held when they came of age. But because it was very expensive a family would often have a combined ceremony for all of their children. So, many whose children were old enough had to postpone the ceremony because they were waiting for their youngest child to grow up.

According to custom, Kadek had to undergo the ceremony in her own home, even though she'd become a member of the nobility. Her parents were going to pay for everything.

'You should have had your tooth-filing done before you got married but at the time I couldn't afford it. Ask the palace's blessing because you must come home for the ceremony,' Kadek's father said.

'Of course you must go home. The tooth-filing ceremony is certainly the responsibility of parents to their children,' Ngurah said when she told him.

'Do I need to ask permission from the palace elders?'

'That would be best. Let's both go and tell them.'

The palace elders gave their blessing but they made a condition: Kadek was forbidden to have her teeth filed on the same platform as her brothers and sister. Because she'd become one of the nobility, she had to have a separate ceremony, on a special platform.

Kadek never guessed that such a formidable condition would be made. It was difficult to accept because it made a distinction between herself and her own brothers and sister. The palace had given her status, a higher class.

'We cannot accept this condition!' her father said. 'You might be having your teeth filed after entering the nobility but you're no different from your brothers and sister.'

Kadek Sumerti had already guessed this was how he'd react. Now she was at the crossroads. Whichever way she went would certainly be wrong; the palace or her family would oppose it.

'You will have the ceremony as the child of your father and mother, Ti, not as someone from the palace. So you must bow to our customs, and not use palace rules in our family. Yes, they give us honour, but we will never surrender our self-respect and be belittled.'

Kadek Sumerti started to cry. When the time for the ceremony drew near, she still hadn't made up her mind whether she would take part or not. Her husband still required her to have the ceremony on a special platform in a separate place.

'You are one of us now, Ti,' Ngurah said, 'and that's why you must abide by the traditional rules of the palace.'

'But you said they were modern people. If they are, why is their attitude so rigid?'

'Rigid doesn't mean old-fashioned. They are defending what they must preserve. They don't want any of their people to submit to or get carried away by outside customs. Modern Americans clearly don't want their people to become like other people. They still want to be Americans. And that's how it is here too. The palace still wants to be the palace.'

*   *   *

Every night Kadek Sumerti could think of nothing else. She had trouble sleeping. If she took part in the ceremony, it meant she'd have to leave the palace and wouldn't be allowed to return. Anak Agung Ngurah Parwata even said bitterly, 'If you do obey your parents' wishes, I'll have no other choice but to divorce you, even though it will break my heart.'

Having her teeth filed on a special platform would clearly be forbidden by her parents. Her father even said furiously, 'If we did that, it would be like consciously accepting an insult to our family.'

She had to make a choice. 'It's up to you, Ti,' her husband said. 'If you decide not to have the ceremony at your home, you can have it done here in the palace some time with members of my family. That would probably be better.'

But suddenly Kadek didn't want to have the ceremony at all. She thought about people who died young before having the chance to have their teeth filed. Then it was done when they were laid out as a corpse. It was a simple ceremony, performed when the corpse was bathed. 'Maybe I'd be better off like them, having it done when I'm dead, even if I am an old woman,' she said to herself.

*   *   *

When the day of the ceremony arrived, Kadek Sumerti left for her parents' home at dawn. Ngurah accompanied her to the palace gates with a blank expression on his face. 'It's up to you, Ti. I hope this isn't the last time you leave the palace. No matter what, we have to surrender to the rules within the walls of the palace where we live our lives and get shelter. I don't have the strength or the power to change that.'

He embraced her at the gates. The morning was still very cool. Birds sang cheerfully in the mango trees in the grounds. The lamps on the terrace had not been extinguished. It was still dark outside. Although Kadek knew what she was going to do, she felt as though she would never return to the palace again.

When she arrived at her parents' home, she saw her brothers and sister busy putting on the traditional costume they would wear for the ceremony. She immediately embraced her mother and father who were sitting watching their three children dressing.

'We've been waiting for you, Ti,' her mother said in a husky voice.

Kadek wept in her father's arms. 'Forgive me, father, but I can't go through with it. Banishment is too heavy a load for me. I'm too young to be divorced.'

Her father stroked her hair. 'Whatever choice you make, we respect it. You are still our honoured daughter and I suppose you are too young to understand freedom of choice, attitudes of modern life, and the complexity of palace life. It's your choice, Ti.'

At the exact moment when the sun appeared in the east, Kadek's brothers and sister in turn had their teeth filed ceremonially in the ceremonial pavilion located in the eastern section of the family's traditional housing compound. They lay on their backs on the platform that was decorated with cloth woven with gold thread and coloured with gold leaf. A priest wearing white clothing and head-dress rubbed their teeth one by one with a file until they were even. The strains of a special song broke the silence of the ceremony which suddenly that morning Kadek felt to be very sacred. The fine hair on her arms stood up on end and her body felt strange.

She stood in a daze watching all the phases of the sacred ceremony from behind a window in the central pavilion. She saw clearly her father and mother standing beside the platform watching over their children till the ceremony was finished.

Kadek Sumerti's eyes were full of tears, her breast was as though crushed between two pieces of iron as cold as ice, and her mind was far away behind the palace walls. Did they realize her heart was in agony, as though it had been stabbed?

A Limited Meeting

SATYAGRAHA HOERIP

Satyagraha Hoerip was born in Lamongan, East Java, in 1934. After tertiary studies in literature, in common with many of the writers represented in this book, he has pursued a professional career in journalism, writing for several prominent newspapers and journals. He has also been head of editorial staff for the publisher Sinar Harapan. He participated in the International Writing Program at Iowa University in 1972–3 and taught modern Indonesian literature and culture at Ohio University in 1982. In 1990 he was visiting research scholar at the Centre for Southeast Asian Studies at Kyoto University in Japan, and in 1994 was a guest of the French Writers' Association.

Satyagraha has written novels, children's stories, and four collections of short stories and edited anthologies of literary essays and a four-volume anthology of Indonesian short stories. In 1987 he won first prize in the Chile Nemis Literary Competition. Satyagraha Hoerip has also written two screen plays, both of which have been filmed.

Many of his stories are satirical comments on hypocrisy and social problems of the times. 'A Limited Meeting', which was published in *Horison* in 1992, is one of these.

'AHAA, I've got it! You're all going to be very pleased with the topic I've thought of!' Budiman Gotama MBA suddenly shouted, like a child. 'Now listen, and you'd better not disagree or I'll murder you, so watch out!'

He leapt to his feet before he'd finished speaking, not even noticing that his tie was caught up in his coat pocket as though a mysterious hand had put it there. His eyes, despite being slit, sparkled with pleasure, and his face, although pock-marked, was radiant. His head, which was starting to go bald, was bobbing up and down as though beating time to rock music.

Seeing his sudden strange behaviour, all of his colleagues in the foundation stared at him. It was strange because Budiman was usually very quiet and never said much at all, let alone threaten to murder anyone.

'What topic? How come your head's bobbing up and down like a rocking horse?' said Engineer Bambang Susila from Malang. In fact, he'd been getting impatient earlier too, but felt he had to restrain himself because he was the host.

For over an hour, the meeting had been at a stalemate, trying to come up with a topic for their forthcoming seminar in five or six weeks' time. None of the suggestions were felt to be very interesting after they'd been looked into. They were irrelevant.

'Come on, Bud, out with it,' prompted Ms Budiati Tarmin LL B impatiently, 'but we're not inviting any more foreign experts.'

'Absolutely not. On the contrary, they all have to be made in Indonesia,' replied Budiman. 'But I guarantee they'll be very interesting. Come on, you can call out the answer. Are you telling me no one can guess?'

His eyes travelled round those present. There were seven of them, excluding himself and the woman taking the minutes. It wasn't until his brain registered again the sound of the air-conditioner in the corner of the room that he realized that the chairman's place was still vacant. Budiman immediately felt annoyed. For as long as he could remember, unless it was his turn to hold the meeting in his own office, it was always the same with Gunadi Ph.D. at every meeting. The invitation would say that the meeting started at 1 p.m. sharp and he wouldn't turn up till at least half an hour later, with some excuse or other. This was in spite of the fact that they often teased him about it.

'That's right, we're not inviting any more foreign experts,' said Dokterandus Yos Parakarta, the foundation's treasurer. 'Don't forget, Bud, at last April's seminar, we lost almost four million rupiah, even though it was a sell-out and the press coverage was satisfactory. Prior to that, we'd never made a loss.'

'I guarantee we'll definitely make a profit this time,' Budiman Gotama MBA retorted. 'Let's get on with it, if no one else has anything to say. Our topic will be "The Message of the People's Suffering", the old propaganda term from Soekarno's day. It will be sure to arouse a great deal of interest, and it will be profitable.'

Budiman got a shock. Everyone burst out laughing except the minute taker, Ms Malia Harun. This attractive, dark-complexioned woman, who was the official secretary of the host, Engineer Bambang Susila, nodded her head. As she looked at the speaker, her right hand was busy taking notes on the pad in front of her. Unfortunately, she wasn't a member of the Guna Bina Foundation. She could agree one thousand per cent and it didn't count for anything.

'Did you say "The Message of the People's Suffering"? … Ha, ha, ha,' said Bambang Susila as his colleagues joined in the laughter. 'You're really something, Budiman. At a time when conglomerates are going into the villages as they are, fancy wanting to talk about "The Message of the People's Suffering". Ha, ha, haaa ... you're a scream!'

'It's so out of date, isn't it?' added Yos Parakarta, which was more or less the same reaction of her other female colleague, Budiati Tarmin, the lawyer. 'Come on now, we've got to be up with the times. We don't want to get ourselves branded as old-fashioned.'

'But that's precisely what is interesting,' retorted the initiator of the idea, sitting down again. 'Imagine if we were to invite Novel Makimbun Ph.D. to give a paper. He can put on a performance as well as a seasoned actor can. I guarantee some of the audience will be in tears. Or yes, the main theme of the seminar could be "Oh My Comrades of the Message of the People's Suffering, Where Were You Silenced?" Now that would be very popular, wouldn't it?'

'Hey, will we hold a seminar or put on a play?' said Marudi LL B. 'I think putting on a play would be a great idea. We've never done that, have we?'

'Yes, a play with an interesting plot would be good too,' Dana Gudilang MA, who'd been quiet up till now, said in support. 'It's the era of *glasnost*, isn't it?'

'That's it exactly,' said Budiman Gotama, 'what is there to hide? They say it's the era of openness, development is spreading everywhere, but isn't "The Message of the People's Suffering" clamouring to be heard? This is an interesting problem. If you just look at the news stories about land, for example, I'm convinced that behind them the people's suffering is on the increase. I'm sure of it. It's just that the intellectuals' voices of conscience have now become still. Because they aren't the ones being evicted from their land and houses, they're falling over each other to keep their mouths shut.'

'Eh, that's going too far,' snapped the host of the meeting, getting red in the face. 'If you say things like that, you're implying things about us.'

'That's not what I'm doing. If our seminar about the people's suffering is a success, it'll provide good campaign material for the candidates in the general election, won't it?'

Everyone stopped talking. Only the sound of the air-conditioner could be heard. And like a snake, Budiman Gotama's idea began to move slowly and infiltrate the brains and steal into the minds of those present, both men and women.

For the next hour, the meeting of the foundation discussed various technical matters. The final decision was deliberately not taken, because they were waiting for their chairman to arrive. From his car *en route*, Gunadi Ph.D. had already let them know that the traffic around the National Monument was totally jammed. A double-decker bus had been destroyed by fire. But he was definitely coming.

Regarding the venue, they thought it should be a strategically located four-star hotel, and even more important, there had to be a very big parking area. Tickets would cost between three hundred and fifty thousand and five hundred thousand rupiah. The invited moderators would receive an honorarium of three hundred and fifty thousand rupiah, and those who presented papers, five hundred thousand. The seminar would run for two days, with the only topic being 'The Message of the People's Suffering', which would be examined from various angles. There would be consideration of its history, its relevance to the struggles of the twenty-first century, prospects for a prosperous and just society as a logical outcome of the message, and so forth.

The Guna Bina Foundation was not a profit-seeking body but their seminars had all been successful in every way (except the last one, but that was because they had invited two foreign experts, one from France and the other from the USA). Despite the financial rewards of their professional organizing skills, they still felt they were serving society.

Their routine meetings were professional. They took it in turns to hold them, unless someone happened to be celebrating a personal anniversary of some kind. Two of the nine members were women, both widows under fifty years of age and principal directors of their respective companies. They had got together to form the foundation through knowing each other at the golf club, because they all enjoyed reading, having discussions, and wanting to do more for society.

'But ladies and gentlemen,' said Engineer Ronggas Siberia, sensible as ever, 'I see some irony here. Think about it. The matter of speakers, that's OK. We'll have some academics, some people with political clout and some experts. But why do we have to discuss "The Message of the People's Suffering" in a luxury hotel where the tickets are so expensive, with participants who are, yes, let's face it, the Indonesian jet set? It's very ironic. And this is not, not, I mean....'

Everyone was annoyed. Although in their hearts they at first agreed with the speaker's reminder, yet they were offended when that Batangtoru man, bold as brass, spoke out like that.

'Yes, ladies and gentlemen, maybe you don't feel it's inappropriate because you are used to luxury living. But I, in keeping with the spirit of the '66 generation, would not really like to see the contrast we are planning here. Good heavens, think about it, will you.'

'"The Message of the People's Suffering" can be discussed by anyone,' replied Budiati Tarmin LL B. 'Isn't it a good thing that those of us who own BMWs and luxury houses, and go abroad like other people go to the Ciplak market, still want to discuss the people's suffering, and how to end it?'

'And that's a sign that we are not traitors, Ronggas,' put in Budiman Gotama, still feeling offended. 'Just remember, most of us here were too young for the student movement actions after the attempted coup of 1965. But nevertheless we want to discuss the people's suffering. That's better than those involved in the People's Three Demands Movement of 1966 who did extremely well for themselves but then said goodbye and left the egalitarian struggle forever.'

The debate went on. The Batangtoru man never backed down, although he was attacked on all sides. The argument stopped when the chairman, Gunadi Ph.D., whom in fact everyone had forgotten about, walked into the room. The cuffs of his pale green, long-sleeved shirt were rolled up. He was wearing a dark brown tie with burgundy-coloured spots. His light grey checked jacket was slung over his left shoulder and in his left hand he carried a heavy leather briefcase. A fragrant scent wafted everywhere, whether from perfume or hair oil no one knew. With a broad smile, he greeted them all, one by one, not forgetting Ms Malia Harun, who was taking the minutes.

It was soon evident that Gunadi was really in charge. After Ms Harun had reported what had been agreed as the proposed seminar topic, it was time to present the set-back: was it appropriate for the people's suffering to be the topic of a seminar, and if it was, wasn't it ironic that the venue would be a four-star hotel with expensive tickets and so forth?

'And don't forget, Dr Gunadi, many of the people whose message of suffering we are going to discuss are still living way below the poverty line today,' said Engineer Ronggas, fidgeting with his fingers.

It looked as though he was worried that their chairman would side with his other colleagues, despite the fact that he was the son of a tobacco farmer in Wonosobo, and so should know enough about the people's suffering. But who knows? There were many children of poor people who, after moving up in the world, really forgot, or pretended to forget, the generosity of the people who helped them when they were still poor.

But Gunadi Ph.D. would not have been Gunadi Ph.D. if he heard such things and then got embarrassed. With his well-known manner—brusque while smiling sweetly—he agreed that Engineer Ronggas's idea was brilliant. They should be grateful to have a colleague who still remembered 'The Message of the People's Suffering'.

'What are you saying, Mr Gunadi?' Budiman Gotama blurted out. 'It was my idea. Ronggas is just objecting to it, don't get it the wrong way around!'

'I am not!' snapped Ronggas. 'I am not objecting to the topic of our seminar, but to the matter of the venue and the expensive tickets. Our programme will surely be a display of idle, bourgeois feudalism.'

'Listen, I want us to open closed hearts, so people will have solidarity again with those who are still suffering. And furthermore, I want them to open their wallets to help those people, or to respond positively when called on to help make a success of community development programmes.' Of course that was Budiman Gotama MBA speaking.

'Right then, ladies and gentlemen,' Dr Gunadi deftly took over, 'we need to remember that discussing the people's suffering is not the monopoly of anyone, and it can be done anywhere at all. If a paper were given, based on the results of fieldwork, which found that in a particular area there was a regional development programme which just made the local people stressed, or poorer, or suffer more, for example, well that would certainly be positive input from us—both for the government and as propaganda for the forthcoming election campaign.'

It was not surprising that Gunadi had previously defended his dissertation so successfully. Although he smiled modestly as he spoke those words brusquely, he had the ability to make all those present nod their heads in agreement. His words were systematic, logical, and persuasive.

In short, that day the Guna Bina Foundation succeeded in taking a unanimous and very important decision. Every member was pleased and happy. The seminar topic was fixed as 'The Message of the People's Suffering', and it would be held in about five to seven weeks' time. It would run for two days, with a total of eight sessions. Papers would be given by officials, and fieldworkers who had just obtained their doctorates practically summa cum laude. There would be three well-known scholars, besides elements from political parties and certain groups, but from the younger generation. The venue would be the Lembusoro Hotel. Tickets would be four hundred thousand rupiah, including morning and afternoon tea, lunch, and a lovely leather briefcase lined with *ikat* woven cloth, containing all the papers, a list of participants, and extensive notes. The suggestion of having a lucky door prize of a return plane ticket from Jakarta to Denpasar had to be rejected because it was considered inappropriate to 'The Message of the People's Suffering'.

Be that as it may, Ms Yos Parakarta was not disappointed. Along with Budiati Tarmin LLB, she would be moderator of one of the sessions, with other moderators of national or even international calibre. She would be sure to be on TV. In her mind, as quick as a flash, she imagined the faces of some of her friends, her couturier, and the top hairdresser in the capital. To them she would willingly surrender herself.

'Ladies and gentlemen,' the chairman of the meeting, who was also chairman of the foundation, said in conclusion, 'today, and with plenty of time to spare, we have succeeded in deciding on a seminar topic which is in accordance with our noble ideals, "The Message of the People's Suffering"!

It is impossible to dispute it. This is the concrete proof that although each of us, praise God, has enjoyed the fruits of New Order Development, we are still close in spirit to our fellow countrymen and women who are still suffering. I hope this is just the beginning and God will be with us. Finally, before we go, don't forget the next meeting will be at Dana Gudilang MA's place at Kuningan in Rasuna Said Street. Thanks to Susila for letting us use his comfortable boardroom.'

He tapped the table lightly three times with his fist. Then looking at Ms Yos Parakarta, who was sitting beside him, he complained, 'My God, I never dreamed that struggling for the people could be so tiring.'

The Chickens

N. H. DINI

N. H. Dini was born in Semarang, Java, in 1936 and emerged as a serious writer in the 1950s. From 1957 to 1960, she was a hostess with Garuda Indonesia Airlines. She has lived abroad in Japan, France, and the United States, and now lives and works as a writer in Semarang. There she also operates, as a non-profit organization, an establishment where children can come and read books she supplies and be trained in writing as well.

N. H. Dini is a prolific and respected writer with many short stories and novels to her credit. Her stories often contain elements of her own experiences or her observations of events that take place in her own environment.

'The Chickens' was first published in the newspaper *Suara Pembaruan* in 1989. The setting is a kampong, a town quarter, and tells what can happen when conflict between neighbours gets out of hand.

'PICK out old, straight bamboo and buy some more if you need it. Make sure there's enough, so when we need some for poles or cross-beams, there'll be a reserve supply at the house. Once the wet season comes, we won't be able to get any more from the village.'

Sumantri gave the worker some money. The fowl pen was finished. Forty free-range chickens of various ages sheltered inside it. The compartments housed appropriate mixes of pairs or families. Every morning they were let out to roam around in the fenced-off yard that was about 25 square feet in area. There they could scratch around for food or hop into the drain. Water from the kitchen always carried grains of rice or other food not thrown away in the rubbish.

Sumantri felt content looking at the realization of his dream. For twenty years, he'd faithfully carried out his duty as a civil servant. In his day there had been no such term as 'lucrative position' which referred to a particular section of an authority where an official could acquire personal financial gain. As an office head, Sumantri was known as a man who walked the straight and narrow path one hundred per cent. He related everything to his own self-respect and he would never ask for anything. He would have been ashamed to accept something he had no right to. He just wouldn't do it. His peers, or those a bit lower in rank than him, could afford brick houses when they retired, but not Sumantri. The wooden house that his parents had owned in the kampong was standing empty, so he took his wife and seven children home there. Because he'd never been a member of any workers' party, his retirement lump sum was intact, almost four million rupiah at the time. When he got it, he went straight to the shops and bought one of the things he'd always dreamed of owning—a colour television set. In the office housing complex where he had lived, he'd been the only one still using a small black and white screen.

Sumantri held steadfastly to an honest way of life. This made him refuse all personal gifts in the form of anything he considered to be too expensive. He did accept food and small items but even those he immediately shared with anyone who happened to be around. He wasn't the sort of boss who never left the office. He knew all the towns on the north coast. He'd once handled the installation of the telephone network to outlying areas. There wasn't a telephone authority tradesman or driver who didn't know his name in those days, because Sumantri never hesitated to climb a pole or haul a cable himself.

After he settled down in the kampong, his home became his office. Never a day went by without his doing some odd job. He always mended anything that was broken himself. The front garden was resplendent with many decorative pots. He and his wife did all the gardening themselves. After the dawn prayer, his first job was to open the doors of the fowl pen. It was at that moment that the inner peace of a man in retirement warmed his heart. He would stand in the middle of the fenced yard, watching his birds that increased in number periodically. He could have four or five eggs a day if he wanted to. The pleasure he felt was very different from anything he'd ever known before. At the kitchen table, he never tired of gazing at the basket piled with eggs. They were so beautiful. Any meeting he went to presented an opportunity to offer the produce from his backyard pen for sale.

He used to be shy about selling things. He wasn't descended from traders or merchants. As far as he knew, his forefathers had always held office as governors, high-ranking nobles, or regents. His own father had been a respected district head. Since he was a child, Sumantri was crammed with ideals of serving his country in the same way. Selling was only done by other classes, not by the descendants of governors and nobles like himself. But, since his tour of duty in Irian, he'd relaxed his strong attitude on such matters. He'd once helped to pioneer the establishment and development of the telephone network in the region that, at the time, had just fallen into the lap of the

Republic of Indonesia. When his superiors asked whether he would go to Irian, Sumantri in turn asked his wife. That mother of seven children whose youngest was only one year old answered firmly, 'We'll go.'

Life in Irian was simple and, at the same time, very pleasant. There were no servants. He had to take care of all household and office matters himself. On the other hand, canned foods, which were a luxury in Java, were easily obtainable there. When ships came into port, people could buy fresh meat and all sorts of supplies. Rice, which was actually among the more expensive food items, was no problem. Sumantri got an allotment from the office and from time to time some shops would sell sticky rice. Sumantri could easily afford all these things on his salary, things he would never have dreamed of if he were in Java. Another thing that was freely available was salt-water fish. Buying fish was like slaughtering a goat. It took a week to get through it all. At the time Sumantri's wife quickly sized up the situation. She realized that the inhabitants of the town, most of whom were Javanese, were used to having certain foods. She was an excellent cook for her family. She capitalized on this and made rissoles and croquettes. She substituted a ragout of the salt-water fish for the filling and added extra spices to disguise the salty smell. It wasn't difficult to find a shop to take what she cooked, but what was difficult was persuading that husband of hers, who was descended from a district head, to carry the food to the shop. However, thanks to her perseverance in overcoming his objections, she managed to get him to do it. Two months passed. It was at this time that Sumantri announced to his wife that his salary was still intact. The family had been able to live on the proceeds of the cooking of the lady of the house. It was only then that the mind of that descendant of governors and regents was opened. Henceforth,

his salary could be used for instalments on a car and a refrigerator. So every morning, with light steps and a beaming
face, Sumantri not only took the children to school, but also
delivered the basket full of all kinds of dishes. When they
went home to Java, they were the only ones in the entire
housing complex who owned a refrigerator.

The satisfaction of settling into the wooden house, which
had been renovated with his lump sum money, was rather
shaken when several of his friends offered their opinions.
Why didn't Sumantri buy his own home? Or why not buy
some land, build a simple house on it, and then let it while
he lived in the house in the kampong? With the money
from the rent, he could carry out improvements. Frankly,
that idea had never crossed his mind. After all, he wasn't
descended from people who were used to calculating profits
and losses. At that moment, he almost regretted that he
hadn't been born into a trading family. However, his rest-
lessness disappeared, thanks to his wife's comforting words,
and they still had some of the lump sum money left,
deposited in the bank for the education of the two children
who were leaving high school. And Sumantri went on with
his hobby of raising chickens. Quite a number of his friends
ordered the eggs. They say free-range eggs are better for
your health. At his wife's suggestion, he divided the pen up
into special sections for pure black or pure white birds.
People often looked for both of these. They were needed to
complete the prerequisites for ritual meals or exorcisms.

Many people thanked God that Sumantri had settled in
the kampong. After the Friday service at the mosque, when
the offerings tin was opened, if there were thousand rupiah
notes, everyone knew for sure they came from Sumantri
and his wife. Their children too were often seen to put in
hundred rupiah notes, even five hundreds. Whenever the
Neighbourhhood Association held door-knock appeals to

raise money for local activities, Sumantri's donation was never disappointing.

The person who benefited most from Sumantri's move was the neighbour who lived at the back of his house. Sumantri didn't regard the repair of the fence separating his house from the row of houses at the back as a matter of great importance. Among neighbours, especially in an urban kampong, what was the problem? Wasn't it a well-known fact that feelings of closeness and mutual co-operation still ran deep in villages and kampongs? Sumantri just bought some panels of woven bamboo for the fence. Then, so it would be strong, he reinforced it with bamboo slats, interspersed with clumps of bamboo that produced leaves that could be used in cooking. For a year, Sumantri wasn't bothered by any of this. He peacefully enjoyed the life of a retired civil servant who was content with his pension of a hundred thousand rupiah and his chickens.

Suddenly, early one morning, he discovered two strange chickens casually walking around in his fowl yard. His own chickens hadn't been let out yet. The sound of cackling made him look up. Three more chickens were perched on the one and a half metre high fence, about to drop down into his yard. From that day on, the cold war that had actually started when Sumantri did his renovations intensified in the form of resentment that obsessed him.

Unlike the other neighbours, the resident at the back of his house was one of the *nouveau riche*. This particular one was clearly created by God to try the strength of the faithful. But it seemed Sumantri had not realized this. When he'd started to renovate his parents' house, an official from the kampong administration office had come to inspect it. He said that the kampong headman had received a report that Sumantri was adding another storey to his house. That would be out of keeping with the rest of the kampong. Did he have permission to do this? Throughout his entire life of public service, Sumantri had always been honest. He knew and obeyed all the rules. Feeling rather offended, he replied that in renovating the house, he had followed the existing system. No permission of any kind was needed. But because the official went on and on, Sumantri's wife, who was looking on, took the hint, and Sumantri was forced to hand over an envelope with money in it for the kampong head. It was only then that he found out from his other neighbours that the man at the back often colluded with the headman. Not long after this incident, just in case Sumantri beat him to it, that *nouveau riche* man extended his house and converted it into a two storey. The new storey was built with iron sheeting and it blocked the view Sumantri had from his yard. The feelings of this retired civil servant who had never deviated from the straight and narrow had now been put under great stress twice: once because he'd bribed someone and again because his view had been blocked. He hadn't yet recovered or calmed down from those things and now he declared that the neighbour at the back was tormenting him with his new chickens. The man had moved to the town but was still acting like a villager. Although he didn't even have a yard, he thought he could keep chickens like Sumantri did and hoped they could find something to eat at Sumantri's place.

Right up against Sumantri's fence, he built a half-pen with a roof low enough for his chickens to jump on to. Sumantri spied on him early in the morning. He watched closely what the birds and their owner did. He heard the man shooing and chasing them. The chickens emerged from behind their shelter and were then herded up to the roof of their pen and from there up on to the fence. When they got there, they were pushed with a broom handle. Naturally they flew down to Sumantri's yard. In the late afternoon, the neighbour called them. Strangely, the small headed creatures obeyed. They organized their journey home by springing up to the branches of the *jambu* and coconut trees that had just been planted, then to the bamboo clumps, and straight on to the top of the fence. Then they vanished behind it.

Sumantri cut down all the branches touching the fence or close to it. But the chickens were just too good at flying. Most of them got out of the way. The younger, less experienced ones hung on and went to sleep in the leaves and branches. Their owner appeared unconcerned. Perhaps he thought Sumantri wouldn't do anything to compromise his integrity. But the bitterness that was building up in Sumantri's heart intensified. He argued with himself: he either had to conquer his pride, give in and talk everything over properly with the neighbour, or he had to do wrong. But was it really wrong? Wasn't there a regulation that if someone else's tree hung over his fence, he had the right to cut down the branches? It's the same with animals, he thought.

Before he'd taken any action at all, a mother hen appeared in his yard followed by eight little yellowy brown balls. They couldn't possibly have got over the fence! Sumantri went over to have a look. Imitating the police on TV, he examined the fence, slat by slat. Ah, there was one broken section wedged with a stone. Only something sharp could have made that section level.

Then the hunt began. He ran around chasing the chickens. Those birds that looked so unworried and innocent proved to be skilful and hard to catch. Sumantri managed to catch a rooster. It was a handsome bird with shiny black and red feathers. He put it in a sack and threw it out on the road. Then he put poison in some food and locked his own birds up in the pen. But the neighbour's chickens wouldn't touch it. They became even cheekier. The little roosters had the nerve to peck and try to break the bamboo pen where his pure white and black chickens were. The purity of the breed was threatened!

That was when Sumantri went to pieces. He got out an air rifle that had been lying in the storeroom for a long time. When evening began to spread its wings, Sumantri took cover. As he waited, his lips were moving, muttering incoherently. One by one, the chickens followed their instincts and started going home without being called. Sumantri raised the rifle. As soon as they reached the fence, he fired. Once, twice, the sound of shots rang out. They missed their target and hit the wall of the top storey. But Sumantri didn't miss too many times. And when the bodies of the chickens fell behind the fence, he grinned. There was a wild look in his eyes that had never been there before.

The House

EKA BUDIANTA

Eka Budianta was born in 1956 in Ngimbang, East Java. After completing high school in Malang in 1974, he studied literature at the University of Indonesia in Jakarta from 1975 to 1979 and from 1980 to 1981 he studied journalism at the Los Angeles Trade–Technical College. As a journalist, he has worked for *Tempo*, for the United Nations Information Centre in Jakarta, and for the BBC in London. In 1987, he took part in the International Writing Program at Iowa University. Much of his creative writing has been poetry, and he has published a number of collections.

'The House' was first published by *Kompas* in 1983, and then republished in a collection of his stories entitled *Api Rindu* [Fire of Yearning] in 1987. This is the story of one of the 'little' people and his desperate longing for that most basic of human needs, a house.

FOR the entire seventy-two years of his life, Marto had never owned a home of his own. That's right, never. All that time he'd always dreamed of a house, a permanent home for his children and grandchildren, but no matter how much he longed for it, it hadn't eventuated. Who knows whose fault it was. Maybe it was because of his meagre wages as a school messenger, or because of fate, or because no one had ever helped him to realize his dream.

Now his three children had given him eight grandchildren and Marni, his eldest grandchild, was about to present him with his first great-grandchild. But Marto still lived in a store shed next to the bicycle parking lot at the school. He'd been there since he was eight years old. At first he was there by himself when he ran away from his parents' home in the village, and then he'd married, had his own children and grandchildren, and he was still there.

He'd served at that school for fifty-four years. He was there in the days of the Dutch when it had been a Dutch Senior High School and he was there now when it was an Indonesian Senior High School. When Marto was young, it seemed the school would provide him with a happy future that would be carefree and very bright. In those days, the teachers often gave him tips and so did the headmaster and even the boys who asked him to help clean their bikes. But suddenly those wonderful days had disappeared.

In their place came the Japanese. The school was closed down and turned into barracks for Heiho, the native militia formed by the Japanese. Marto was thirty years old at the time and it brought a terrible tragedy for him—his oldest son was shot dead by the Japanese. Mardi! He was only nine years old. Marto nearly didn't go back there again. He swore he'd leave the place forever. But no matter what he said, he was only a powerless human being and he had not been able to keep his own oath. With three small children and a wife who was ill at the time, he was forced to continue his life in the four by six metre store shed. He went on working as a messenger and also doubled as a gardener.

Now Marto was tired of dreaming. When he was young, he'd drawn up all sorts of plans, designs, drawings, and specifications. Once, in the time of Soekarno's Guided Democracy, he even tried asking the headmaster for a loan, but he was refused.

'Forget it, Marto,' the headmaster said at the time, 'or there'll be other problems, maybe worse. I suggest you be patient. After all, you've got a nice place to live now. It's healthy, and close to the school, and it doesn't cost you anything.'

Starting round about that time, his wife opened a small cake stall. The business was actually very promising at first. The cakes became so popular that Marto fantasized that before long he'd be able to open a cafe or maybe even a restaurant. But all that was twenty-four years ago. Now it was 1983. The stall was just the same as it had always been and the restaurant he'd dreamed of hadn't eventuated. He still didn't even have the house that had started to seem a real possibility, let alone a restaurant.

He wasn't eligible for a pension because in fact he wasn't a public servant. He just worked at the school in return for accommodation. It was impossible. Once he'd registered for cheap housing with the National Housing Authority, but he had no luck and finally gave up. He couldn't even afford to rent a place somewhere else, let alone buy a cheap house. The only thing that sometimes gave him some consolation was the poverty of the vagrants. There were many people, from the time they were children until they died, who didn't have a house. A child would be born homeless under the Ciliwung Bridge and would still be there at the age of sixty-five. Looking at that sort of thing, Marto was consoled a little. He was better off than the people who only set up shelters of cardboard and plastic along the railway tracks and river banks. But he still had his beautiful dream. Sometimes it took the shape of scribbles on paper, calculations of costing, and plans, complete with the furniture he planned to have. But it never got any further than that.

Everything ran into the brick wall of acquiring money. Plans to borrow from various sources always failed. He got no support. Sometimes he had a close relationship with the children at the school, very close, but only for three years at the most. All he got was just a tip or a packet of cigarettes. He once heard of a man who got rich quickly because of an inheritance. But what legacy was there for him? He'd broken off with his family and relations. His father-in-law was a soldier—clearly there'd been nothing from him. Buying lottery tickets? He'd tried many times. He'd spent a lot but never struck it rich.

The peak of his longing had been the previous week. He had read a short story about a man who managed to get some money by writing a letter to God. The story told how the man had complained to God about his financial problems. His children were ill and he was very poor. Marto laughed when he read that the letter finally attracted a donation from the postman. At first he was amused and laughed at the idea, but gradually it dawned on him that perhaps he could get a house the same way. Maybe a postman or a policeman or someone else would be moved and lend a hand to help him in God's name.

So, on Monday evening, nervously and with his heart pounding, he plucked up the courage to write a similar sort of letter to God.

'Dear God, I am really embarrassed to write a letter like this,' Marto began. He regretted that he hadn't been the one to think of such a letter in the first place. 'But it can't be helped. You know what's happened to me all this time. You've seen how I've wanted a house of my own since I was very young, how I tried to save up, how I tried everyone for a loan and some help.

'I understand, God, a house is a worldly matter, a need that has nothing whatever to do with spiritual life and may even endanger it. Perhaps if You had given me a house long ago, our relationship wouldn't be as close as it is now. Maybe a house would have become a kind of obstacle to my devotion to You. For example, I might have been too busy looking after and maintaining it, and not had enough time for my prayers. Maybe also if I had my own house, I might have committed sins that I couldn't have if I didn't have one.

'I don't understand, God, how even though a house can bring danger for people, I still long for one. I've always prayed for one. You must know how many thousand nights I've spent making novenas and praying. Now, I'm seventy-two years of age, my eyes are dim, I'm bald and I'm very weak. I can't understand it myself. I'm sick and tired of continually wanting to have my own house. I can't stop thinking about it, my own house which would become a family home to pass on to my children and grandchildren.

'Now, God, this may be the last time I ask You for anything. Through this open letter, I am knocking on the door of Your heart, and asking You to shower blessings upon me in the form of a house. It's up to You what sort of house You give me. Anything will do. I no longer want a small house with a big yard or a two-storey house like I used to. I don't care if it's beside a main road or in a village. Provided it is habitable, can be called a house, and becomes mine, I'll accept it and be grateful to You.

'Possibly my reasons aren't good enough and I can't move You with my words. Or perhaps I can't convince You of how terrible my longing is to own the house of my dreams. You know about my aspirations, my calculations, and my madness. I'm sure that You, Almighty God, know all this. You also know what house would be right for me— what sort of house, where it is, and when I will get it. It's all in Your plans, of course. I know I can't suggest anything about all that to You.

'But, God, You also know how urgent my longing is. I'm obsessed with wanting my own room and my own bed, wanting to close my own doors and windows, and feeling the pleasure of having my own home. You know how I feel, how I've suffered, sleeping in that store shed for fifty-four years. You know how it has tortured me. You know when I was chased away, when I didn't get on with the headmaster, when I had arguments with some of the teachers. You know it all, there's really no need to tell You.

'Now, I don't know how You're going to do it, God, but please grant my request. You have millions of ways of making contact with humans; through millionaires who feel compassion, for example, or charity from the community, or gifts from the President. Whatever and however, I want to have my own home, now.'

With his feelings in turmoil, Marto set off determinedly to post the letter. He regretted being unable to write a moving letter. He felt he couldn't even move the heart of a postman, let alone convince God. Despite the fact that he felt that his letter was the most beautiful and best thing he'd ever written in his whole life, he realized that. He was sad and felt stupid and crazy and annoyed with himself. But he hoped, and perhaps he was deceiving himself too, that the letter would elicit a good response from God, no matter who, or in what way, someone was touched. He knew perfectly well that the letter wouldn't reach heaven, but in any case the first postman who read the address would have a good laugh.

He walked from the school to the post office. It wasn't far, just about six hundred metres. His mind, his heartbeat, his breath, his vision, even his actions seemed to be floating. It wasn't like walking along on asphalt, but like speeding along among the clouds. It was as though his body no longer felt the force of gravity. He was light, as light as an inflatable doll filled with helium.

'Marto!'

'Yes, God.'

'Where are you going?'

'To post a letter to You, God.'

'Why are you doing that?'

'I need a home, God, and I need it now.'

'Why can't you be patient, Marto?'

'I've been patient for too long, God.'

'Very well. I have actually already prepared just the right home for you.'

'Have you really, God?'

'Yes, I have. Come, Marto, follow me.'

'Thank you, God.'

Marto followed God and disappeared behind a cloud.

Three Important Gentlemen

BUDI DARMA

Budi Darma was born in Rembang, Central Java, in 1937. He obtained his degree in the Faculty of Literature at Gadjah Mada University, Yogyakarta (1963), and his MA (1976) and Ph.D. (1980) from Indiana University in Bloomington, USA. He was recently a Fulbright Scholar at the American Studies Research Centre, Osmania University, Hyderabad, India. Budi Darma is a lecturer at the Teachers' Training College in Surabaya, East Java, where he has also served as head of that institution. One of Indonesia's most respected authors, Budi Darma has been writing since the mid-1950s. He writes novels, short stories, and literary essays, and has won various literary prizes, including the ASEAN Prize for Literature in 1984.

'Three Important Gentlemen' was published in *Horison* in 1988. The author uses the technique of the absurd to tell a story of strange relationships between men and one particular woman, and of the power struggle between them.

ONE day, in a certain small community, a man went home from work much earlier than usual. He strongly suspected that his wife just lazed around and slept while he was away.

He went inside, and angrily headed straight for the bedroom, the only one in the house. He was right, his wife was asleep. Choking with anger, he dragged her out of bed by the legs, and she crashed to the floor. Wiping her eyes, she got to her feet and sat at the foot of the bed.

'So, this is what you do every day while I'm working hard,' snapped the husband.

'If you work so hard,' said the wife, 'how is it that you can't support me properly?'

'I'd work a lot harder if you gave me a child,' the husband said.

'Don't you put on that act,' said the wife. 'Which one of us is sterile?'

The husband regarded his wife's body unhappily.

'Because you're sterile and you can't support me, you make out it's my fault that we can't have children.'

The husband went out and sat in the adjacent room, the only other room in the house.

'If you dropped dead, I'd soon prove I can have children,' the wife snapped from the bedroom.

Naturally, her husband heard her. Furiously, he got up and left the house. Hearing his footsteps, the wife hurried out after him. He stopped.

'So you hope I drop dead?' he asked.

'I'm going back to bed to dream of it,' she said.

He left the yard without looking back. His wife went straight back to bed and fell asleep immediately.

Who knows why, but at the corner of the street, the man collapsed, twitched a few times, and then died.

A death that wasn't all that interesting became so because the man's wife was considered to be the best-looking woman in the whole district. And that pretty woman who'd suddenly become a widow wouldn't have attracted so much attention if there'd been any eligible men around. But because all the men were already married, the question on everyone's lips was how was the woman, whom everybody knew to be lazy, going to support herself?

Naturally, all the married women secretly began to suspect that she might trap their husbands at any moment. A few of them even swore they'd cold-bloodedly burn their husbands alive if their suspicions turned out to be correct. Of course, they could go on with such nonsense because their husbands were just ordinary men. If they'd been very important men, it would have been a different story. If the wives had tried anything like that, their husbands would have beheaded them. In that district, the ancient law that wives of important men couldn't do anything without their husband's permission was still in force. Now it so happened that there *were* three important men in that community.

Time passed. While the man who'd dropped dead suddenly was increasingly forgotten, his widow was increasingly noticed—because she was growing more beautiful. The attention really reached fever pitch when it became obvious that she was pregnant. Everyone was aware that more than just a few months had passed since her husband died. The baby in the widow's belly was certainly not his.

All the married men felt deprived of their freedom because they were under their wives' surveillance. What was very annoying was that any husband who managed to escape his wife's scrutiny always bragged that he was the one who'd made the widow's belly swell. Because every adult male considered that this was a manly thing to do, secretly they each competed to be considered the most virile. Whether they'd impregnated the widow or not wasn't the issue. The main thing was that they each wanted to be thought solely responsible for it. They were competing fiercely for the reputation of most virile man in the village.

Of course, in any competition, the strongest man will win, and in bragging about themselves, the three important men were well to the fore. They were each known to be virile, to be hot-tempered, and to have a lot of authority. And they each had a unique characteristic that made them even more notable. The first man had very big eyes, the second had very big ears, and the third had very big hands.

Time passed and the widow's belly grew larger and larger.

'If the child has big eyes, then it proves I'm the father,' boasted the man with the big eyes.

'You're wrong. How could a widow as pretty as that possibly want to have sex with you?' the man with the big ears blustered.

'You can go on arguing,' the man with the big hands bragged. 'You're both going to be disappointed because the pretty widow's baby will definitely have big hands.'

All the other men, who felt it was no use bragging about themselves, surreptitiously followed their argument.

One day, unexpectedly, the widow vanished. All the wives felt happy because they didn't need to keep an eye on their husbands any more. The men also felt happy because they could do whatever they wanted to, without being followed by their wives. Only the man with the big eyes, the one with the big ears, and the one with the big hands felt disappointed because no one took any notice of them now. Secretly, they each cursed the widow and prayed day and night that she would drop dead and never come back.

One day, out of the blue, she did come back, carrying a baby who had big eyes, big ears, and big hands. Immediately, the wives of the men with the big eyes, big ears, and big hands were furious with their respective husbands. Confronted with the widow's baby, they forgot that their husbands were important gentlemen. Fortunately, they didn't go as far as lashing out at their husbands in public. But they were delighted when they heard people jeering that none of the three could justifiably claim to be the most virile.

Quite by chance, one day the three men ran into each other at the spot where the widow's husband had dropped dead nine and a half months previously. They glared angrily at each other. They were so busy doing this that they didn't realize that everyone had come to see what they did next. Their wives turned up briefly, then unobtrusively went home because they didn't dare rebuke their husbands, especially in public. Now there remained the spectators who had no interest whatsoever except to stickybeak. Nevertheless, they all secretly hoped that the three important gentlemen would attack and kill each other. If they were eliminated, then the chance of all the onlookers being able to gain some kudos would increase.

Suddenly, the three men got a big surprise and so did the spectators. The widow appeared carrying her baby.

'When my husband died, you were pleased because you were free to sleep with me,' she said. 'But after you got what you wanted, you forgot all about providing for me and my child. I'm warning you, anyone who fools with me will surely die.'

'Don't you accuse me of making you pregnant just because your baby has big eyes,' said the man with the big eyes, glancing at the widow, and then at the other two men in turn.

'None of my ancestors had big ears,' said the man with the big ears, 'so if your child has big ears, it doesn't necessarily mean that a big-eared man made you pregnant.'

He shot a quick look at the pretty widow, then the baby, then the other two men.

'As a respectable man, I was once interested in making you my mistress, pretty widow,' said the man with the big hands, 'but as a man with a sharp nose for scandal, I was not prepared to share you with these two.'

He glanced briefly at the widow and her baby and glared at the other two men.

'Very well,' the pretty widow said, 'I'll show you that I can support myself and my baby and uphold our dignity.'

The widow left and so did the three men. Everything was calm as if nothing had happened. How each of the three men felt no one knew.

The calm atmosphere didn't last long. The widow's baby died suddenly, and nobody knew why. The married women got worried again in case the widow went looking for another victim after failing to trap the three important gentlemen. Would she compensate for this failure by snaring some other man—it didn't matter who—as long as it was a man? Meanwhile, all the men started to feel overwhelmed because their wives' eyes always followed them everywhere. Secretly, they still wanted to be considered virile too, so the rivalry that had died down for a while revived again.

The ones that suffered most among this small population were the three important gentlemen. As soon as the widow's baby died, they each felt incredible changes take place in their bodies. A short time later, the man with the big eyes went blind, the man with the big ears went deaf, and the big hands of the third man became paralysed. Their wives were secretly pleased because these misfortunes freed them from the possibility of being abandoned.

News of the inexplicable disaster that struck them spread like wildfire. The three men felt they didn't deserve to suffer such a blow and in their hearts each one blamed the others. Without telling anyone, they set out from their respective houses to pick a fight and were not going to be satisfied until they killed their enemies.

Because he'd lived in that district all his life, the blind man had no trouble heading for the houses of the other two. Steadily, he walked to the corner of the street. At that moment, the man with the big ears was also heading for the corner to get to the houses of the other two, and the man with the big hands was doing the same. By coincidence they all reached the street corner where the widow's husband had died, at the same time.

Suddenly, out of nowhere, a large vehicle appeared, heading for the corner. It was the only time such a vehicle had ever passed through that place. Although it was thundering along loudly, the man with the big ears didn't hear a thing because he was one hundred per cent deaf. And the man with the big eyes was startled because in his whole life it was the first time he'd heard such a loud noise. Being totally blind, he couldn't work out where the noise was coming from. And the man with the big hands suddenly lost his balance because in fact he wasn't yet used to his hands being paralysed. Meanwhile, the big vehicle kept coming fast. And after it ran down the three important gentlemen, it sped on.

Sita's Holy Water

LEILA CHUDORI

Leila Chudori was born in Jakarta in 1962. This story was first published in the newspaper *Kompas* in 1987, and then republished in 1989 in a collection of her stories entitled *Malam Terakhir* [The Last Night]. Leila Chudori has been writing since she was a young girl, and was a journalist with the news magazine *Tempo* until it was recently banned. She studied at Trent University in Ontario, Canada, and Canada is the setting for this story. In it the writer juxtaposes what is happening in the real world of the main female character as she waits for a visit from her fiance after a four-year absence, with what is happening in her imagination as she pictures scenes from the Hindu epic, the *Ramayana*, where a king is reunited with the wife from whom he has been parted for a number of years. There is a clear feminist perspective as, through her character, the writer questions the prevalent double standards of sexual mores for men and women.

SHE had the sensation that night had suddenly crashed into her, sending her reeling. She stared wide-eyed at the darkness around her, feeling stunned and anxious.

So, night is here at last, she thought bitterly, but there was no nobility in the way it arrived. Night should replace dusk, which merely mediates between day and night, in a gentle, feminine way. Because of its gentleness, the creatures of the earth should feel the faint coolness brought by the change in time. But because night had come upon her as it did, she was confused and did not know how to react. For the first few moments, she was stifled by the unwelcome night.air. It's so hot and sticky, she thought, dabbing the beads of perspiration that were starting to soak through her dress.

She heaved an anxious sigh. Earlier, she'd received a long letter from her fiance. Now it seemed that some kind of power from his letter was pursuing her so that she felt short of breath. She could not imagine how she would face her fiance if he were to turn up right at that moment. In the stifling heat and discomfort of the hostile Peterborough summer, his letter brought her no joy.

Four frozen years, she thought, suddenly imagining the knee-deep Canadian snow. Four years of being strong and never lowering her defences.

Sweat trickled on to her brow and ran down her pale temples. He, her fiance, wouldn't be able to comprehend that body and soul she was still chaste and pure, despite contending with the sixteen changes of season she'd spent in Canada. He won't understand. He won't believe me. He'll keep his blinkers on when he judges me, she thought, stung by paranoia.

Her whole body was tortured by the awful, stifling heat. God, it's so hot I'm burning up, she thought angrily. She got a glass of cold water and sipped it slowly, looking out of the window.

Night, she thought with a shudder, despite the fact that the sun was shining brightly. She didn't even hear the shouts of the little children from the flat next door playing with water. She could hear another voice, loving and commanding. Then in her mind's eye she saw the face of the mighty King Rama, an incarnation of the god Visnu.

'My wife … you know there is no reason for you to doubt my great love for you. We have been parted by a raging, endless sea, so vast that a band of loyal friends had to build a bridge across it to reunite us. Nevertheless, my love, bridge or no bridge, the fact remains that you were in that evil, alien place for a long time….'

The mighty king did love his wife. However, after she was abducted by the ten-faced demon king, he no longer spoke about that great love. He was more interested in dwelling on the fact that his wife had stayed so long in a strange land. He was more concerned about her purity and he doubted her strength.

It's so hot, she thought miserably, thinking of the scene that had just been enacted in her imagination. Even husband and wife can still mistrust each other….

She ran to the bathroom. Moaning hysterically, she turned the cold tap full on and then stood under the shower with her eyes closed as the water drenched her. When she emerged from the bathroom a short time later, she didn't bother changing her sopping wet clothes that were clinging to her body.

She glanced out the window and slowly became aware of a scene that claimed her attention—her neighbour's children, naked, playing with water. Their pale bodies glistened in the sunlight. They were squealing and yelling as they took turns to hose each other, and she could hear their mother shouting at them to stop. Then it dawned on her. It's still daytime, she thought with surprise.

*   *   *

'Will you sleep with me?' The man spoke intimately with a slight tremble in his voice.

Strangely, she wasn't the least bit angry, as she thought she should be. She looked at the Canadian quizzically. She couldn't believe what he'd just said to her.

She went to the door, opened it, and stood there with a disparaging smile on her face.

'Are you telling me to go?'

'There's nothing more to discuss,' she replied, trying to compose herself.

'Is this the loyalty of Asian women that everyone admires so much? Why won't you sleep with me?'

'Why? Because I will not sleep with a man who isn't my husband ... believe me, I mean what I say.'

'God, doesn't it mean anything that we love each other? That we've loved each other for two years?'

The woman opened the door wider. The Canadian just stood there dejectedly, shaking his head.

'Good night.' She kissed his cheek and he walked away with sagging shoulders.

'Oh God ... !' she moaned, leaning against the door.

*   *   *

It's so stifling tonight. The flames are torturing me again, she screamed inwardly. She imagined the demon king approaching the beautiful goddess. Was he always wicked? Was he really as evil as the composer of the epic portrayed him? How did he behave when he tried to get close to the goddess whom he had abducted? Had he been rough, or had he shown a man's gentleness? But the fact that the goddess was still pure in the end proved how he'd behaved, didn't it?

The woman was again overwhelmed by paranoia. Although her 'lover' had never touched her, she felt she had entered the domain of the ten-faced demon king.

My God, what if my fiance had suddenly turned up on the doorstep that time when my friend was trying to get intimate with me? What would have happened? she thought, letting her imagination run wild. The first thing my fiance would do would be to kill him. Then, because he'd suspect the worst of me, he'd recite a litany of accusations about my infidelity. Like the great King Rama, he would spout pearls of wisdom about his undying love and affection, comparing his love to an endless sea, a limitless sky, and so on and so forth. But then, as is the case with a person who, in the eyes of society, comes from a religious background (her fiance did come from a very devout family) he'd say, 'Nevertheless, my darling, even though it's just a formality, for the sake of my reputation as a religious man, it's natural that I should ask you about your fidelity, your purity, and your restraint. In permissive Western society, people have sexual relationships as easily as they buy vegetables at the market. It's reasonable then that I should ask you some questions about the four years we've been apart....'

His words would pour out like water gushing from a broken dam. The torrent of words would be more like accusations than questions so that she'd drown because she couldn't offer any defence. Defence? Would she have to defend herself? Would she have to prove that although she had a close friendship with the Canadian man he'd never even touched a hair of her head? Shouldn't the truth be self-evident without having to be defended? But would her fiance be astute enough to discern the truth and her innocence? After all, the great King Rama still expected his wife to plunge into the sea of fire to prove that the demon king had never touched her.

Now the woman felt that she was the one floating in a sea of fire. The clock struck three times. The occupants of the flats were probably all sound asleep. It was so still and quiet. She couldn't stand it a minute longer. She had to escape from the sea of fire. She ran to the bathroom and again stood under the shower. Her whole body and the clothes clinging to her were saturated. She stood there for a few minutes with her eyes closed. The faces of her fiance and the great king alternately imprinted themselves behind her eyelids. 'My love, my darling ... for society's sake ... for the sake of my reputation ... for the sake of.... '

*   *   *

'Excuse me, was that you having a shower last night?' asked the old woman whose flat adjoined the woman's bathroom.

She nodded slowly. 'I couldn't sleep because of this dreadful heat. I'm sorry, did I disturb you?'

'Oh no, no. I was just wondering. By the way, what about your fiance, is he still coming to visit you?'

The young woman leaned against the wall of the hallway and uttered a deep sigh.

Surprised, the old woman said, 'You look pale, dear. Are you ill?'

She shook her head quickly. 'No, no, I'm fine. I'm expecting him this evening. I'm probably just over-excited,' she said and quickly disappeared behind her door.

Shaking her head, the old woman chuckled, 'Young women are like that, they always get agitated when their prince is on the way'

And back in her room, she really was agitated. She was beside herself. It's happened again, she thought. Night has swept down on me and wilfully overpowered my day. It's forcing me to suffer this unbearable heat. And she dashed to the bathroom again and sought relief under the shower and stood there for hours. And hours....

*   *   *

'My darling ... you look so pale and tired,' her fiance said, gathering her tightly in his arms. 'Didn't you sleep last night?'

She nodded listlessly. 'It's this awful heat.'

'But you feel so cold and icy. And look at you, your fingers are all wrinkled … have you got a fever?'

She shook her head and quickly pulled herself together. 'Would you like some tea or coffee?'

'Let's have some later. Come and sit down. I want to feast my eyes on you …,' and his eyes took her in from head to toe.

'I guess we've got a lot of catching up to do about these past four years,' he went on, gently taking her hands in his.

But her hands suddenly felt frozen. It's time for the trial to begin, she thought resignedly.

'You know, darling … for an engaged couple like us, being separated for four years is hardly an ideal situation. It's only natural that there have been trials and obstacles along the way, a bit like deep pot-holes and steep hills.'

He's off to a diplomatic and sweet start, she thought, staring at her fiance's face, which was looking more and more like the face of King Rama.

'We both knew there was a possibility we'd have to cope with things like that. What we must do now is to look honestly at the facts, that is, at what sort of obstacles we've come up against these past four years … why don't you say something?'

'I can't think of any….'

'Darling, I know you've been steadfast and strong and pure. But the truth is that I've … failed you…,' he stroked her cheek, his eyes glistening with tears. He seemed to be very emotional. 'What I'm trying to say is that now we have to look openly and honestly at what's happened….'

The woman frowned.

'I know that you've been strong confronting the hazards of the past four years. But you are a woman, and women usually have much more strength and self-control than men.

A woman can stay dry in a raging storm. A woman can still remain strong after climbing a mountain no matter how high it may be.'

She listened, spellbound.

'But I'm a man, and it's common knowledge that we men are damnable creatures. We aren't nearly as strong as you women when we face hills that aren't even very steep or pot-holes that aren't very deep. When we're tempted, the fact is we're rarely prepared to be rational. Because we're supposed to have such a strong natural sex drive, we're spoiled. Society gives us free rein to indulge our sexual desires, without any need to feel that we're guilty, or behaving badly, or betraying anyone. Darling, I've been a terrible fool, and like some men when they've been unfaithful, I feel like a filthy, contemptible traitor. You've been so pure. I can't tell you how small I feel. I can't understand what got into me during these past four years away from you. I can never forgive myself and I....'

The woman was looking at her fiance's lips that were so preoccupied with himself. Yet all she saw were the faces of Rama with his wife Sita, who was ready to plunge into the sea of fire to prove her innocence. She suddenly thought of something. Sita had never been given the opportunity to ask her husband any questions, such as 'My husband, while we were apart, were you ever tempted to be with another woman?'

Such a question was never uttered, and there was absolutely no suggestion that it should be. How strange....

And now, slowly and courteously, night crept in.

The General

RAY RIZAL

Ray Rizal was born in West Sumatra in 1955. When his father, a policeman, was posted to Riau, the family went too, and Ray was raised and did his schooling there. On finishing high school, he went to a teachers' training school in Padang, then taught for two years at a junior high school in West Sumatra. In 1978 he moved to Jakarta to pursue a career in journalism. He is currently a journalist and editor of an arts and culture column for the weekly magazine *Mingguan Mutiara*, and has won awards for journalism and for a literary essay. He has written a number of books of children's stories, and has had four collections of short stories and a biography of the artist Affandi published.

'The General' is taken from the collection called *Dalang* [The Puppet Master] published in 1991. The story is about an old former freedom fighter, labelled as mad, who lives among the poor and homeless social outcasts in Jakarta.

ALMOST every day the tall, well-built man was there at the large intersection, not far from the overpass bridge. He stood on the footpath right at the end of the lane from the south that headed north to the city. Every time the traffic-lights went red and the cars stopped, he started marching up and down, holding himself erect, like an officer inspecting a guard of honour.

In his left hand, he held a baton, which he sometimes tucked under his arm. His behaviour was like that of a general. From the medals made of bits of tin hanging from the lapel of the old dress coat he wore, and the row of four stars made of bottle-tops attached to the shoulders, it was easy to guess the state of his mind. His hair reached to the nape of his neck, its tangles covered by the peaked cap he wore perched on his head, while his moustache and beard were long and unkempt, giving him a frightening appearance.

The traffic-lights turned green.

'Hi, General!' shouted a passing driver.

The man who'd been called 'General' raised his hand in reply. He seldom smiled, let alone laughed, as though displaying the qualities of a real general with a resolute character. He hardly ever said a word to the people around him.

The street traders and homeless people who congregated under the overpass bridge didn't know where he came from before he began operating there. No one even knew his name. He'd just raise his hand or occasionally wave if someone called him General. No one even remembered who first gave him that name.

The drivers of cars that were held up at the lights often tossed small change to him. Some did it because they were scared of his baton, or worried that he might throw stones at them, but most of them regarded what he did as free entertainment while they waited for the lights to turn green. They didn't mind giving him small change.

After sunset, the General dropped in at a food stall under the bridge. His two cats welcomed him, going up to him and purring. One, a white one, nimbly jumped up on to his lap, and the other, a black one, licked his hand. They had learnt the habits of the General, who would give them a fish each.

'Don't be so lazy,' the General muttered as he stroked their heads. 'You're only purring to get food. Typical animals.'

His words greatly amused the people who heard him.

'You mustn't be like human parasites. They might be alive but their souls are dead. You must work honestly and loyally,' he said, patting the cats' backs until they nearly choked.

What the General said to the cats was just like a father's advice to his children. The people who had laughed earlier now started to question whether he really was mad. From his appearance, it was clear that he wasn't normal, but the words he spoke didn't suggest madness at all. Was it only because he wore a strange and unique uniform that he was shunned as a madman? Weren't there many people who were sane in theory, but whose behaviour smacked of madness?

After his meal, the General stood up and groped in the bulging pockets of his coat. Coins could be heard chinking. The woman who owned the stall told him how much he owed and the General counted out the exact amount for her.

'Freedom!' the General shouted, waving his fist.

'Long live the General!' replied the stall owner, restraining her amusement. There's no harm in having a bit of fun, provided I don't lose customers, she thought.

She didn't really care if the man was mad or not. The main thing was that he didn't disturb the peace and drive away her customers. Besides, people who were healthy in mind and body often ate and drank at her stall and went off without paying and she made nothing at all for her efforts.

The General seemed to obey the work ethic. You worked for what you got. He often said this to his two cats. The cats didn't understand him but the people who heard

him often thought he was insinuating things about them.
But they didn't dare ask him and didn't know how to. The
General's conversation was all one way—there was no
dialogue. Every time someone tried to ask him a question,
he just giggled or muttered incoherently to himself. No one
even knew what language he was speaking—maybe it was a
mixture of Padangese, Batak, Menadonese, Ambonese,
Javanese, Sundanese, and Acehnese.

'He's not all there, you know,' the stall owner said,
tapping her forehead with her fingers.

So people just watched his antics from a distance and
kept their questions to themselves. Wearing his uniform of
high office, he crossed the road with sure steps.

'General!' shouted a group of children on their way
home from school. The General spontaneously turned and
waved a few times.

When the lights turned red, he started his routine. He
saluted every car. Some people threw money at him and he
deftly caught it, sometimes scrambling under the cars to get
it. Then he briskly saluted again and moved on to the next
car. Some of the drivers and passengers ignored him. They
didn't even look at him, let alone open the windows and
throw money out.

When the lights turned from amber to red to green, the
General put on his show. Now and then, he looked at the
sky and saluted the heavens. What his actions meant, no
one knew, except himself in his own strange world.

When he was worn out from all his hard work, he
headed for the place where he slept under the bridge. There
he was free to doze or sit back and look around. His eyes,
which were sometimes wild and sometimes dull, watched
the heavy traffic and the people passing by. No one knew
what was in his mind as he watched the medicine seller
surrounded by crowds of people, or the junk dealer, the

shoe mender, the barber, and all sorts of people who took advantage of that strategic spot to display their wares. The huge, solid area under the bridge functioned as a makeshift market that held a lot of customers. The vast, soaring concrete served as a roof to protect them from the rain and burning sun. Coolies could rest there comfortably, unemployed people could take it easy, and it was a shelter for the homeless.

The General was absorbed with his cats. He leaned back against the iron struts of the bridge and the cats wrestled with each other and licked his feet and hands.

'You're always in a hurry to lick my hands when you're hungry.' His loud laughter could be heard, echoing in the space. He hugged the cats affectionately. 'Don't worry. We'll have something to eat soon. Even without licking me, you'll certainly get some fish. After all, I rescued you from the rubbish tip, so it's my job to look after you,' he informed them.

When night time came, the cats slept curled up with the General, under the bridge, together with the homeless. They slept soundly and peacefully, even though up on the overpass, cars kept racing by all night long until morning.

*   *   *

On the day the anniversary of independence arrived, the General's appearance was a bit different. He'd tied a piece of red cloth around his head and wasn't wearing his cap. He'd replaced the baton with a bamboo spear and he looked solemn and different from usual. He stood right in the middle of the intersection. His left hand held the spear in a vertical position and his right hand executed perfect salutes.

'You useless idiot!' car drivers shouted angrily, because they had to slow down to avoid him.

In no time at all, there was a traffic jam. The General
reminded people of the statue of the unknown warrior.

'You crazy old freedom fighter,' more abuse was heard
from other drivers. But the General continued to stand
motionless at attention. Beads of perspiration ran down his
face. His body, wrapped up in his heavy coat, was boiling in
the sun's heat and drenched with sweat.

Suddenly, from the direction of the traffic jam, a motor
bike appeared, ridden by a traffic policeman. He rode
up to the General, who was standing stiffly to attention. At
first, the policeman was loath to speak to the General. For a
long time, he'd been allowed to play his role, because he
was doing no harm. But this time he had to be spoken to.

'Excuse me, sir, you're causing a traffic jam,' the policeman said respectfully.

Faced with the General wearing the trappings of a
freedom fighter, a spear in his hand, four 'stars' on his
shoulders, and 'medals' on his breast, no wonder the policeman felt uncomfortable.

The General turned his head to look at the policeman.
His eyes were as red as the seeds of the *saga* tree. The
policeman's guts contracted. He didn't dare do anything
rash. Questions piled up in his mind. Was this man crazy or
was he really an ex-freedom fighter? Say he *was* crazy, it
would be very risky to do anything because of the bamboo
spear he was carrying.

'Can't you see the traffic getting jammed, sir?' the policeman asked, trying to be patient. But it appeared the General
wasn't easily softened with words. The policeman had to
wait for a sign from him. At the same time, he was weigh-
ing up the best thing to do. Would he have to use force and
handcuff him?

'Where's the traffic jam?' the General suddenly said. The
authoritative voice made the policeman's heart pound. He

felt strange facing the fact that a madman had charisma. And stranger still, it seemed as though it really was a general standing there facing him.

'Indeed, you can see it for yourself, sir,' the policeman replied softly in a low voice.

'Where is the source of the trouble?' asked the General in a heavy, deep voice.

'It's because you're standing right in the middle of the intersection,' the policeman answered quickly.

'Ha, ha, ha,' the General laughed, 'it's not me causing the traffic jam. Cars cause traffic jams. Cars crowd everywhere. Order them to line up—one, two, one, two, ha, ha, ha.'

The General marched on the spot with his feet stamping.

'I must ask you to move aside, sir, because many people are on their way to the Independence Day commemoration ceremonies and they'll be late,' the officer said trying to coax him.

'Right. Very well, I'll carry out an inspection. Forward march, one, two, one, two.'

The General marched up to the cars one by one, with his hand raised to his head in salute. When it was the turn of the fifth car from the front, he pulled up with a start. Through the open car window, the face of an old man sitting inside was clearly visible. The old man was craning his head and smiling as he watched the General's actions.

It was hardly credible, but all of a sudden the General howled like a wounded tiger and with all his strength he hurled the spear. His aim was accurate. The old man in the car writhed as the spear was embedded in his chest. His eyes started in pain and his body was bathed in blood.

'I've waited a long time for this. I've been searching for you for years! This is the day of vengeance! Damn you, you traitor!' the General shrieked and shouted and ran along the road.

People panicked. The traffic was in chaos. The spear had claimed a victim! Now the General snatched a pistol from under his shirt and brandished it wildly. Everyone was shaking with fear and feeling threatened. Suddenly, three shots rang out. Who else had been killed?

With three bullets buried in his body, the General staggered, then collapsed. Blood soaked his uniform, the four stars on his shoulders, and his medals. His eyes were shut tight and there was a peaceful expression on his face. The policeman's bullets had found their mark. With confused emotions, he picked up the General's gun which had threatened people's lives.

It was only a toy pistol.

The Madman

AGUS FAHRI HUSEIN

Agus Fahri Husein was born in Singaraja, Bali, in
1964. He completed his tertiary education in the
Faculty of Literature at Gadjah Mada University,
Yogyakarta, specializing in Javanese literature. Since
1981, his literary output has included essays, short
stories, novelettes, poetry, and tele-drama scripts. He
has also worked as a journalist and is currently editor
of religious, social, and philosophical books for a
publishing company in Yogyakarta.

Agus has won competitions for creative writing and
this story, 'The Madman', was selected for inclusion in
an anthology of poetry and short stories published in
1992 under the auspices of the Fourth Yogyakarta Arts
Festival. The aim of the book was to highlight the
work of a new emerging generation of writers. The
story depicts the tensions and effects of the gambling
fever that sweeps through a poor village when a
government-sponsored lottery is introduced.

KAMSO the village headman walked around the foundations of the lime kiln he was building. There was still a long
way to go. He could just imagine how the people in his
village would flock to work there when it was finished.
There was an abundance of limestone in the barren hills

where the village was situated. Farming was almost impossible there. Limestone was the only raw material around that
could be processed. Through his lime kiln, the village co-
operative would make a nice profit, the people would make
a living, and he hoped his village would soon lose its label as
the poorest in the district. Kamso smiled to himself with
satisfaction, then left the foundations, and made his way to
Parni's stall for a cup of coffee.

As usual, Parni's was crowded. It was especially so on
Wednesday nights. Ever since the government-sponsored
lottery had been introduced, it seemed as though the people
had nothing better to do than try to predict winning numbers. Kamso could only feel sad and helpless. He estimated
that at least two million rupiah of the villagers' money was
being swallowed up every week by those white tickets. In
his capacity as village chief, he'd once tried to trace their
source but he gave up after he uncovered the fact that a
certain uniformed element was behind it all.

As village chief, Kamso tried to do his very best for his
people. Now his own savings were dwindling because they
were being used for the lime kiln, and he was powerless to
stem the flow of funds draining uselessly out of the village
away from the people. The most he could do was just warn
them individually, and even that was limited to the people
close to him, such as Uncle Parmin.

'Come on, Uncle, you have to think of the future.
Instead of throwing your money away on tickets, you could
be saving quite a lot …,' but before he'd finished speaking,
Uncle Parmin suddenly cut him short.

'But that's what I *am* doing. Every Wednesday night.
That's my future, don't you see, every Wednesday night.'

Chief Kamso could only grimace when he heard those
words. His face felt hot. He quickly finished his coffee and
left the stall. He was worried about a recurrence of his high

blood pressure. He thought of reporting the situation in his village to the subdistrict head or the regent, but when he remembered the uniformed person, he dropped that idea.

As time went by, things in the village grew steadily worse. The foundations of the lime kiln came to a standstill. Kamso had no more money. He actually wanted to conscript the villagers to finish the job but didn't have the heart to do it. Every day, they went down the hill to the town to work as coolies or at some other hard labour and were exhausted by the time they got back in the afternoon. Meanwhile, the activity generated by the lottery tickets increased. There was no conversation without numbers being mentioned. Furthermore, the people now started behaving very strangely. They connected every single thing that happened to numbers—no matter whether it was a collision, a flood, or an earthquake. Moreover, when someone won, and admitted that he'd got the numbers from the graveyard, crowds of villagers went off to spend the night there, hoping to receive some divine inspiration.

The climax came when a crazy tramp strayed into the village hall. At first, only the younger children, who teased him, took any notice of him. But a week later, when another person who won admitted that he'd got the numbers from the tramp, people crowded on to the veranda of the village hall where he was camped. Chief Kamso just watched it all from his office window. He saw the madman signalling with his fingers to the people around him, then roaring with laughter.

The next week four men won and all had picked numbers given to them by the tramp. The village hall became even more crowded. Food to feed the tramp arrived from the winners and because he felt it was required of him, his behaviour became increasingly bizarre. He scattered some cakes that someone had brought him on the ground, bleated like a goat, got down on all fours, picked up a cake in his mouth, and ate it like an animal. Then he stood up grinning and pointed at someone in the crowd.

'Do you want some numbers?' he asked as he went on pointing.

'Yes, yes, I do,' the man he pointed at replied.

The tramp then threw another cake up in the air and on to the ground. He laughed again, then suddenly his eyes bulged.

'Well, you eat that like I just did,' he snarled at the man, who was a bit scared and backed away a couple of paces.

'Do you want some numbers or don't you?' the madman asked, in a whining voice like a little child.

The man looked to his left and right and his friends egged him on. Then suddenly he crawled over to the cake, picked it up with his mouth, and ate it.

The tramp laughed and jumped up and down, pointing in all directions. Then when the man who'd just been on his knees stood up, the tramp signalled with his fingers. The man jotted something down on a scrap of paper, then ran home to the sound of his friends' laughter.

Such was the scene every day on the veranda of the village hall, and every Wednesday night, there were always winning numbers. The villagers became even more idle. Actually, the fact was that thanks to winning tickets, a few people were able to repair their homes, and some put their winnings to work and got into trading. But most of them squandered their money on high living, alcohol, and chasing after women.

Word had it that in this one month, the lottery agent had to pay out twelve million rupiah in prize money in the village, and the amount would keep growing. It was always certain that when the agent came, he would be bringing winnings.

So the mad tramp became more and more like a king. His wish became the people's command. It was said that some of them even brought in prostitutes for their mad lord and master. For days, all Kamso did was keep watch from his office window. He had to admit that the tramp had brought about an improvement in the economy of the village with his accurate predictions. But was that enough reason for the village to depend on a madman? All of the chief's efforts to bring the villagers to their senses were in vain. Several young preachers that he brought from a couple of Islamic associations went home feeling very embarrassed. The congregation in the village mosque on Fridays dwindled to half. Chief Kamso didn't dare do anything rash by confronting the people who were so obsessed with the lottery. One false step and they could go berserk. That's why all he could do was think, without taking any action at all.

But that last Thursday, there was uproar on the veranda of the village hall. The mad tramp was found dead, with his neck almost completely severed. Blood was spattered and congealed all over the floor. Apparently, he had suffered a long death agony. The blood on the floor looked like mud that ducks had scratched around in.

More and more people came crowding around, jostling each other to get a glimpse of the blood-smeared corpse. Some screamed when they saw it. Some young children stood trembling, ashen-faced after looking at it, and their mothers hurried them away from that awful place.

Kamso heard people asking each other who could have done such an inhuman thing. The atmosphere became tense when someone said, 'Who else but the lottery agent? He certainly didn't want us to keep winning all the time.'

Then like a swift flowing stream, the crowd suddenly surged towards Parni's, where the agent was spending the night. The human current was unstoppable. Wild shouts accompanied the moving mob.

Kamso the village chief smiled thinly, watching it all. He thought back to what had happened the previous night and how his hand had trembled as he swung the sword to cut the madman's throat.

The Men Who Laughed

YANUSA NUGROHO

Yanusa Nugroho was born in Surabaya, East Java, in 1960. He completed his education in Jakarta, taking his degree in literature at the University of Indonesia. His poetry and short stories are published in *Kompas*, *Horison*, and other mass media, and two anthologies of his short stories have also been published. Yanusa is currently working as a copywriter in an advertising agency, and continues his creative writing career.

'The Men Who Laughed' was published in the anthology entitled *Bulan Bugil Bulat* [The Round Naked Moon] in 1990. Many of Yanusa Nugroho's stories tell of the lives of people from the poor stratum of Indonesian society. This poignant story presents us with a glimpse of tiny parts of the lives of some of these people, contrasted with the life of one wealthy family, in Jakarta.

HE stepped over some rotting wood lying across the track, and pain shot through his hip. He drew in his breath sharply. His dry, peeling lips trembled and his open mouth revealed two rows of dull, yellow teeth. Beads of perspiration trickled down his face. That one short step had been as difficult as if he were carrying the weight of a water-buffalo.

He leaned back against a pile of rubbish, and went limp, as
though the tension had drained out of him. His eyes were
closed and his mouth sagged open. His right hand rested
loosely on the rim of a broken plastic bucket and his left
hand was folded across his stomach. The flies that had just
flown away because they were startled by the old man now
came back buzzing and feasting around the carcass of a dog.
But now there were even more of them because there
would soon be extra food—a decaying man. His chest rose
and fell weakly with his breathing.

*   *   *

Not far from the pile of rubbish, which was in the town
garbage dump, was a kampong settlement. The mountain of
garbage and the settlement were separated by a small,
brown river that ran between them. On days like that one,
usually when they got home from school, Acin, Budi,
Wawa, Maman, and sometimes Ai bathed and went swimming. It was the best way of cooling off. Completely naked,
these primary schoolchildren would jump and dive from the
iron bridge which no one used any more because it was
rusted. Their shouts of laughter would shatter the silence of
the heat of the day.
    Like that day.
    'Wa, I'll race you, come on!' Acin challenged.
    'Let's go!' shouted Wawa.
    They both stripped off their shirts and pants.
    'But we better swim on our backs!'
    'OK! Come on, one, two, three!' Together, they jumped
into the water. They swam with their shining faces turned
up to the blazing, hot sun.
    'Damn it!' yelled Wawa a few minutes later.
    'What's up?'

'I got a handful of poo,' he said crossly, but then laughed as he saw the funny side of it.

They swam over to the bank without bothering about their race, got dressed and disappeared, swallowed up by the decrepit huts in the kampong.

*   *   *

Further along, the river flowed past the backyards of a luxury housing complex. There could be found small kingdoms surrounded by high walls, and at almost every front gate was the threat: beware, savage dog.

Later that afternoon, in one of those houses:

'Nem, is the boss at home?' a man called Ramli asked the servant.

'He's just gone out with the missus. What do you want?'

'It's like this,' Ramli said, drawing near, 'I need my money. My wife's got a fever, and tomorrow I've got to take her to the doctor,' he said expectantly.

Nem didn't answer. She looked blankly at Ramli.

'The boss didn't say anything about it,' she said sadly.

The sound of a piano in the living-room filled the silence of the late afternoon in the kitchen. Soon it started raining.

'The prawn chips are still outside drying! Wait a minute, Ramli!' Nem ran out to get them.

Ramli didn't comment. It was as though he'd reached a dead end. Nem came in and put the chips on the table.

'He promised he'd give it to me today,' he said, protesting against the harsh reality that the afternoon had brought.

'He's busy, he's got a lot on his plate. Yesterday, he had a fight with the missus. You know what he did, he threw a whole dish of rice as big as this on the floor.' She bent her arms as though she were carrying a barrel.

Ramli didn't say anything. His mind was on his wife, who since the night before had had a high temperature which still hadn't gone down.

'This morning they were all lovey-dovey and everything was fine again.'

From the living-room, someone called Nem, and she hurried away. Without saying goodbye, Ramli slipped out the back door.

Heavy rain fell on him, drenching him and freezing his sarong. He didn't try to run or find shelter. When he stepped on the bamboo bridge that linked the two sides of the river, the boss's car entered the garage. His wife was happily carrying a large box, containing some purchase or other.

Ramli crossed on over, and meanwhile the rain got heavier. Meanwhile too, the old man who was in the rubbish dump moaned softly for a few moments, then his body contorted and went rigid. But Ramli didn't hear anything. He slipped between the walls of the huts, sometimes ducking to avoid colliding with the roofs. He just smiled in answer to the greetings of some of the owners who happened to see him.

'Have you been at the river?' asked Bejo, his neighbour.

Ramli nodded.

'Did you see Maman?'

Ramli shook his head.

Bejo complained angrily about his son.

*   *   *

The rain got heavier and the water started rising. If it didn't go down quickly, there'd certainly be a flood. The rain and wind howled and whipped around as though spilling out from a huge water jug in the sky, which was emptying itself on the earth's surface. The water rose higher. On the highway, it was already knee-deep, overflowing and flooding the park and the shops around it. It was now difficult to distinguish between the small river and the ground to the right and left of it. It was full, level, brown and thick with mud. There were intermittent claps of thunder that sounded like a whip being cracked to make the rain fall faster.

Inside his house, Bejo put a chair on top of a table and climbed up to fix the tiles on his roof that had slipped out of place.

'Tun, did Maman come home from school earlier?' he shouted crossly, trying to keep out the rain. His face was wet from the dripping water.

'I don't know!' his wife replied.

'What?'

'I don't know!' she yelled again.

Bejo got down, wiping his face with his singlet.

'You're supposed to look after him,' he grumbled bitterly.

'Well, you were here, what were you doing? Don't just blame me. All day long, all you do is day-dream and think about your other woman all the time,' his wife retorted just as bitterly.

'You shut up or I'll thump you!' Bejo threatened angrily.

Atun held her tongue and went out the back to get on with her work.

'When he knows his son's not home, specially when it's raining and flooding like this, why doesn't he do something about it? He's the father, isn't he? All he does is just get angry,' Atun could be heard complaining from the back of the house.

Bejo didn't say anything.

*   *   *

The water was a quarter of the way up the poles supporting the watchman's shelter at the end of the kampong. That meant that the right bank of the river was totally under water. And when that was the case it meant the water in the housing complex was waist-deep.

'This is great, we can play boats.'

'Give me some paper, and I'll make one,' Maman said, clutching his school-bag.

Budi got his exercise book, tore some paper out without a second thought, and gave it to Maman. Maman took it, made a few folds, and fashioned a paper boat. They were having a wonderful time. They didn't care about the flood or their parents worrying at home. Since the rain had started earlier, they'd been sitting up in the shelter.

'Our boat's off to America, yipee!' Budi yelled excitedly.

The paper boat soon got wet bobbing up and down, and was swallowed up by the muddy current. The boys made another boat, and another, and another.

*   *   *

'Nem!'

'Yes, missus!'

'Is the back door shut?'

Nem remembered that it wasn't. She ran to the back quickly. Water was already inside, up to her knees.

'Nem!' called her boss.

'Yes, sir?' Nem climbed the steps again.

'Lock the front door!'

'Yes, sir.' Nem ran to the front, hitching up her sarong, whereupon the master had a good look and the mistress caught her husband gazing at Nem's lovely legs.

'Nem, what are you doing that for? Don't tell me you're frightened of a bit of water,' her mistress scolded and then wandered upstairs after her husband.

Nem got drenched locking the front door and then ran to the back where Bruno was getting wet from water which had reached the floor of his kennel.

'Nem, bring Bruno inside, here's an umbrella,' Miss Dita called from the upstairs window, tossing the umbrella to her. Nem, who was already wet, caught it. When she opened Bruno's kennel, he jumped into the water. Nem just gawked at him and Miss Dita shouted abuse. Bruno swam into the kitchen. Nem tried to catch him to lift him up, but slipped and fell over in the water, dropping the umbrella.

*　　*　　*

From the mosque came the call, 'Let us pray!'

*　　*　　*

When the paper boat went under and surfaced again, part of its triangular sail got caught on the finger of a human hand. But Maman and Budi didn't notice. Maybe they were both busy making more boats, or maybe they couldn't see because it was getting dark. Hand and boat bobbed around dragged by the muddy current, up and down like the evening prayer call being swallowed by the rain.

*　　*　　*

Ramli nursed his youngest child, trying to comfort him so he'd be quiet. His wife opened her eyes a moment, then reached out her arms to take the little one. Ramli handed him over. On the soles of his feet, he could feel the cement floor of his house starting to get damp, and meanwhile the rain didn't let up.

Next door, his neighbour Bejo and his wife started quarrelling again about Maman, who still wasn't home. The wife was crying and Bejo was panicking.

Ramli just listened to the noise, his own breast assailed by a storm of confusion.

'Did you get it?' his wife asked softly.

Ramli just sighed.

'What did they say?'

'That I shouldn't have been late and now it's a lot of trouble to get my pay,' Ramli muttered pouring out his anger.

'What are you going to do?'

'Him and his cement walls along the river bank! He might be rich but he's a mean bastard,' he swore angrily.

*   *   *

At six-thirty, suddenly the rain eased and soon stopped completely, leaving a cold stillness. The sound of music came from the transistor radio in Sarpan's stall. At Bejo's house, Maman could be heard crying from the hiding his father had given him. Bejo and his wife seemed to be taking it in turns to vent their anger on the boy.

The water went down quite quickly. Nem had started opening the doors to drain it out. Her mistress stood upstairs glumly with her hands on her hips. She could be heard complaining over and over at why they'd moved to that district.

By nine o'clock, Nem had finished mopping up and cleaning the floor which had been covered with mud and all sorts of filth.

'Did you put some disinfectant on it?'

'Yes, missus,' Nem answered, heading out towards the back.

'Well, how come it still smells!' her mistress criticized, then went back upstairs.

Nem didn't reply, and went out to lock the back door of the kitchen. But she'd no sooner reached it than she stopped in her tracks. For a moment she couldn't believe her own eyes. Quickly, she turned on the back light and....

'What's the matter, Nem?' called her mistress, who was startled when she heard Nem's frightened scream from the kitchen. She hurried downstairs.

She saw Nem sitting stock still, her face pale, unable to speak. Unconsciously, she followed Nem's blank stare and she too screamed with fright and then fainted. The master and Dita flew down to the kitchen. Dita supported Nem and her father carried his wife out. A moment later, he came back to the kitchen and had a close look around.

His eyes fell on a human shape lying face down at the foot of the back door. The left hand was stretched out as though scratching the earth of the yard, and caught on its finger was a torn, paper boat. The master was startled but quickly took control of the situation.

After he closed the kitchen door, he telephoned the police and the hospital.

'How's your mother?' he asked Dita, who didn't answer.

'Phone Mr Wahono next door, or get on to someone, Dita, quickly.'

Dita, who was very confused, did what her father told her.

'Nem, where's Ramli?' he asked angrily.

Nem just kept crying.

'That's enough. Shut up! They're never here when you need them, only when they want money ...,' he grumbled to himself.

Not long after, several police cars arrived, followed by an ambulance from the hospital. Bruno started barking and Mr Wahono's dog followed suit. Mr Wahono went outside and other close neighbours also came out to see what was happening, while those further away just peeped out of their upstairs windows. They all stood around talking quietly.

'Where's the headman of the kampong?'

'They're sending for him, sir.'

They went on discussing the corpse.

'Who on earth is he?'

'Goodness only knows, I don't. The gentlemen will take care of it, or maybe those kampong men there.'

'Yes, I suppose so.'

'Hopefully, they'll find out who he is, or perhaps the headman knows.'

*   *   *

Maman was still getting over his recent tears. He was sitting on the corner of the sleeping platform huddled up in his sarong. Earlier he hadn't gone swimming with Acin and Wawa. He and Budi went to his Uncle No's place in the adjoining kampong. Uncle No asked them to sell some kites for him. They got twenty-five rupiah each for every kite they sold and that was their pocket-money. But unfortunately that day the kites weren't finished. They had to go back the next day to get them. Maman wanted to earn his own pocket-money without telling anyone. But his explanations to his father earlier seemed to have no effect at all, so Maman concluded that no one was interested in his efforts.

*   *   *

Ramli, Bejo, Kirman, Boing, Sarpan, Ending, and a few kampong officials followed the headman to the housing complex.

'Did someone get drowned?'

'That's what they say.'

'Who is it?'

'Nobody knows.'

When they got there, they saw the face of an old man with his gaping mouth full of mud. People just stared at the body lying on the stretcher. They speculated and made guesses, and then worried. Some of them told stories about members of their family, friends, and friends' friends who'd drowned in wells, rivers, and so on. All sorts of stories came out but still didn't shed any light on the identity of the old man on the stretcher.

'Are you sure he's not one of your people?' a policeman asked the headman.

'I'm positive. I know everyone in this kampong.'

The police quickly gave orders for the body to be taken to the hospital and the ambulance roared away. The police cars left too. The neighbours went back to their homes, and the boss went back inside after having a few words with Ramli. Nem was still hunched up with fright in the pantry.

*   *   *

On the way home, the headman's party went on chattering about the drowned man.

'I feel sorry for the poor old man!'

'Maybe he was relieving himself and the flood came and he didn't have time to get up, and he got dragged under.'

'What was he doing, relieving himself in the rain?'

'I suppose he couldn't wait,' someone answered with a laugh.

'When you've got a pain in the guts, it doesn't matter if it's raining, or if it's hot, when you've got to go, you've got to go,' someone else added, chuckling.

They all burst out laughing.

'No, I reckon he wanted to sail away in his boat,' someone said.

The others stopped talking a moment, as though they were remembering the paper boat which earlier they'd glimpsed caught on the dead man's finger. At the time they'd wondered about it but didn't want to be considered stupid by linking the paper boat with the dead man. But now the story was embellished and turned into a great joke.

'Maybe he wanted to sail off overseas.'

'Where to?'

'I don't know. Maybe to Holland or Japan!'

In the cold of the night, they all roared with laughter.

A Roast Chicken

GDE ARYANTHA SOETHAMA

This story was published in 1993 in the Sydney-based Indonesian language newspaper, *Aquila*. A roast chicken and uncompromising adherence to tradition become the focus of conflict between two brothers.

'COME on, let's just take it, Tom!'

'Do you think we should?'

'Use your eyes! Aunty Nyoman's already sprinkled the holy water and taken the incense away. That means the offering can be eaten. What are we waiting for?'

Toma was still doubtful. He looked at the roast chicken again. It certainly looked tempting in the beautifully arranged offering. It had a coating of yellow turmeric and the brown skin roasted over the coals had been sliced open from the neck to the stomach. Then it had been arranged in a standing position and encircled by flowers, cakes, and fruits such as *salak*, apples, mangosteens, bananas, oranges, rambutans, and mangoes. Aunty Nyoman herself had arranged the offering, and it had been specially placed on a table in the middle of the yard on a length of black and white checked cloth that looked like a chess board. Once the offering had been made to Hyang Widhi, it meant it had been accepted by God and anyone was free to eat it.

Since earlier in the day, Toma and Dedi had been think-ing about the chicken. They hadn't taken their eyes off it, frightened their cousins who'd all been taking part in the holy day ceremony at the family home since morning would beat them to it.

'Come on, are we going to take it or not?'

'I'm scared, Ded!'

'Fancy being scared of an offering. Father said the offer-ing must be eaten all up because Hyang Widhi has enjoyed its essence. We should just be grateful because we'll enjoy God's blessing.'

Finally, Toma was persuaded. He stood up and walked slowly towards the table. His hands were shaking and his heart was racing.

'It's all clear, Tom, it's safe, go on.'

In one swipe, the roast chicken was removed from its position. Dedi took the prize with a suppressed shout and the boys crept inside and started eating straight away. The chicken's neck had been tucked in so it would be easy to set it up on the offering.

But just as Toma took a bite of the crisp tender breast, he heard Aunty Nyoman screaming in the middle of the yard, 'My God! My roast chicken! My roast chicken!'

That scream startled everyone. They all hurried into the middle of the yard. Those who were performing prayers at the shrine cut their prayers short. They pulled up with a start when they saw Aunty Nyoman's pale face.

'My offering has been ruined! My roast chicken's disappeared.'

'Maybe a dog ate it.'

'A cat could have run off with it.'

'Don't worry about it, Man. You've already offered it to God, haven't you?'

'Yes, yes, I have. But why has it disappeared? I can't see any signs of a dog or cat running off with it.'

Toma and Dedi stopped chewing and looked at each other. Then Toma pulled out a newspaper from under the table and spat out what was in his mouth. He grabbed the meat that Dedi was still clutching and wrapped it all up. They wiped their lips and went outside, feeling very worried.

* * *

Putu Darmika saw the incident as the beginning of a huge disaster. When his brothers and sisters said it was a minor matter, Putu was furious. When they giggled at Aunty Nyoman flying into a panic because she'd lost her roast chicken, Putu glared and his jaws moved as he gnashed his teeth.

'This is a curse!' he cried to everyone present. 'We have to atone for the missing chicken.'

Atoning for something that went wrong when performing a traditional and religious ceremony was no simple matter. Later that night, Putu announced that a special, large-scale ceremony of appeasement would be held.

'We can't concern ourselves with whether the chicken was taken by a dog or a cat or deliberately stolen by someone. What's clear is that it was taken without the permission of the owner,' he said. 'This is extremely negligent. We have to apologize to Hyang Prama Kawi and our ancestors because we've done wrong. We must have the special ceremony, otherwise disaster will befall the family.'

Nobody dared to comment. When it was a matter of traditional customs and religion, Putu's opinion could not be disputed. For the past five years, since their father died, everything concerned with traditional matters had been entrusted to him. As the oldest brother, whatever he wanted had to be obeyed. He'd become very authoritarian. If anyone dared to oppose his opinion, he always snapped, 'Do you want our grandchildren to live under a curse?'

So a family meeting decided to hold the appeasement ceremony. It was estimated that preparations would take two months and would involve everyone in their community organization. Dozens of chickens and ducks would be slaughtered and some buffaloes, cattle, and a special striped dog. About three hundred kilograms of pork would be needed for the offerings and the feast for the people of the community group. All this would cost three million rupiah which would be raised from contributions from each family.

Toma and Dedi were terrified when they heard the decision.

'We have to tell father,' Toma said. 'We've got to tell him the truth, that we ate the roast chicken because we didn't know the rules.'

It was true that the two brothers didn't know much about the proper conduct with regard to offerings in ceremonies. They were actually born in Bali, but spent their childhood and adolescence in Semarang in Java. Their mother was Javanese, from Cirebon, and their father had opened a printing business in Semarang. For the past three months, he'd been commuting between Semarang and Denpasar because he planned to start a printing business in Bali. When a special holy day ceremony was arranged at the family shrine in Bali, Dedi and Toma were invited to come along. They were pleased to meet their relatives and see the colourful offerings. Their mouths watered when they saw the roast chicken on Aunty Nyoman's offering.

Their father, Ketut Lasia, was dumbfounded when he heard Toma's confession. 'Why have you waited till now to tell me?'

'I was really scared. I didn't understand anything.'

'But the family has already decided to hold the ceremony and your uncle Putu won't want to change anything.'

'But there's nothing wrong with you explaining to them, father.'

*　　　*　　　*

Ketut finally went to his older brother. He intended to say that the roast chicken had been eaten by Toma and Dedi, and not taken away by a supernatural creature as almost all the family thought. He hoped that as a retired teacher, his brother would have the sense to call off the ceremony that was causing so much fuss and costing so much.

Ketut tried to tell the story as slowly and clearly as possible so that Putu Darmika would relent.

'I ask your forgiveness, brother. My sons have done something very wrong. I realize this is because we've been away many years from the family traditions. They don't know anything about them.'

Putu Darmika did not speak. Ketut bowed his head, looking at the edge of the chair. He was aware that he had to be very humble facing his brother, the most rigid man he'd ever known.

Then Putu said, 'Do you realize it's your fault? Your fault as head of a family that only chases after money in someone else's part of the world and never teaches its children about the traditions of the land of their ancestors?'

Ketut kept his head bowed. He understood there was no need to answer the accusation.

'If the wrongdoing only affected you, it wouldn't concern me. But when it's a family disaster, I must decide what has to be done about it.'

'But you know they're still children, they don't know anything yet.'

'Your sons are in senior high school. Children here of the same age know about correct behaviour and tradition. They are instructed in religion, customs, and ceremonies. They learn obedience and are given a lot of discipline. Toma and Dedi aren't children any more. You must direct them to learn our customs because they are the inheritors of them. I really cannot accept your excuse.'

'They're about to start. They're going to university in Bali. They'll become Balinese. But I beg your forgiveness because they've done such wrong. I know the consequences are very serious.'

'The guilty have to be punished. That is our tradition. No one who does wrong gets off scot-free. You know that.'

Ketut took a deep breath. He knew his brother's heart was hardening. He'd always been so rigid.

'But you could explain to the family what really happened.'

'Of course, I'll explain, but I will not cancel the ceremony.'

Ketut sighed. He'd come to Putu to persuade him to call off the ceremony because the problem was clear. For Ketut, it was a case of why waste so much money, time, and energy on a mistake made by children who didn't understand?

'You do know what this ceremony is for, don't you? It is so that the balance of our world will be maintained. This ceremony is important so that we are always in bonds of harmony. It is not a case of wasting money, Ketut.'

'Normally, I would agree with you, but not in this case. Especially when it's going to cost so much.'

'Of course it's difficult to talk about ceremonies, traditional customs, or religion with someone who's a business-man. You should know that the appeasement ceremony is a ceremony of holy sacrifice. We must do it wholeheartedly. You should not consider the cost of it in terms of profit and loss.'

'I understand that. But I feel it's wrong and useless to have the ceremony for the sake of a roast chicken that my sons ate.'

'What are you saying! There's nothing wrong or useless if we perform a holy sacrifice! Absolutely nothing!' Putu shouted bitterly. His face was getting very red and Ketut realized he had to end the argument quickly. There was no way of changing his brother's mind. The retired teacher was at the peak of his authority as the oldest in the family.

'In that case, I'll leave. Once again, I apologize because Toma and Dedi did something wrong which has to be atoned for at great expense to the family'

'I'm grateful that you recognize your mistake. But I must remind you that however small the wrongdoing in our customs, it must always be punished. We cannot avoid it.'

Ketut looked at his brother's face. There were no signs of friendliness. It was a face that he didn't know at all now.

'You must atone for your sons' error, Tut.'

'I'll be glad to. Tell me how.'

'You must pay all the costs of the ceremony.'

Ketut was staggered. His chest tightened. The chair he was sitting on was like a bed of coals.

'I feel that is right because it is your sons who are the cause of all this trouble.'

'But you must put this to a family meeting.'

'I don't feel that's necessary. No one will refuse if you guarantee the expenses of the ceremony. They're sure to agree. And indeed they must accept my decision.'

Ketut went outside slowly. As a businessman, he could afford it but why should he spend such a large amount of money for the sake of his children's misunderstanding, which was clearly all the problem was?

'Only in Bali could a roast chicken cost three million rupiah,' he muttered under his breath.

Typical

Putu Wijaya, who was born in Bali in 1944, is one
of Indonesia's best-known writers. He studied Law at
Gadjah Mada University in Yogyakarta and became a
member of W. S. Rendra's Bengkel Theatre in 1968.
Later, he established and now heads the Mandiri
Theatre in Jakarta. He is possibly the most productive
Indonesian author, writing short stories, novels, novel-
ettes, plays, and poetry. He has won many literary
competitions for his work, including the ASEAN
Literary Prize in 1980. A collection of his short stories,
entitled *Bomb*, has been translated into English, as
have other individual stories. He participated in the
International Writing Program in Iowa in 1975–6,
performed at the All-World Theatre Festival in Nancy,
France, in 1975, and was a guest lecturer at the
University of Wisconsin in 1985–6.

'Typical' tells of how friendship is perceived in different ways by a Balinese and a Westerner and how
this affects the expectations they have of each other.

WAYAN had been invited to Jakarta by a European friend
who was leaving Indonesia and going home. The friend was
paying his fare and providing meals and accommodation.
He wanted to shake hands with Wayan for the last time
because it might be a long time before he returned to

Indonesia. He didn't have time to go to Bali despite the fact that Wayan had written many times that he wanted to say goodbye.

This white man and the Balinese man had been friends for a long time. They'd met a few years earlier when the white man was holidaying in Bali. Wayan had given him a lot of advice and enjoyed taking him to see interesting things off the tourist track. They had become close friends.

'It will be terrible if I can't see you before you go. We've been like brothers even though our skins are different colours. You've eaten and slept in my humble home and you're just like one of the family to us. I'll feel guilty if I don't get the chance to see you before you leave. So if you can make it, please try and come to Bali. I can't possibly come to you because I can't afford it and I'm tied up with some of our traditional ceremonies,' wrote Wayan.

John was touched. He put his hand in his pocket and bought a plane ticket for Wayan. But when he arrived, he wasn't alone; his nephew was with him. Wayan admitted that he was scared of coming to Jakarta by himself. 'After all, this was my first plane trip and Jakarta is so big I'm frightened I might get lost.'

John was surprised. He hadn't counted on this, especially as far as his budget was concerned. On the trip from Cengkareng airport to Kebayoran Baru, Wayan mentioned several times that he borrowed the money for his nephew's fare and was worried about how he was going to repay it.

'It's OK, don't worry about it. I'll take care of it,' John ended up saying. He didn't want his pleasure at seeing Wayan spoilt. 'But how long will your nephew be staying in Jakarta? I haven't got another room. There's only one spare room and you'll be using that.'

Wayan answered quickly, 'That's no problem, John. We'll share. We're used to five in a room.'

John pretended to smile but he wasn't happy. He knew that Cambodian refugees could live with tens of families in a makeshift shelter but that didn't mean that he, as the host, would like it. He'd have trouble sleeping if there were two people using the single room, especially when one of them wasn't welcome and he'd been forced into putting him up.

What finally upset John more was how preoccupied Wayan was with looking after his nephew. The nephew didn't keep him company, it was the other way around. Wayan totally forgot that he'd come to Jakarta to say good-bye to John and his only topic of conversation was all sorts of trivia about his nephew. He never asked one single question about how John was, when he was leaving, what he was going to do in the future, and so on.

John felt cheated. He started to hate the nephew and ended up resenting Wayan too, because it was clear that the friendship John imagined through the letters all this time amounted to nothing. Wayan obviously had no interest at all in him. 'He must have just put on a show of friendship to trick me into giving him a free ticket to Jakarta,' John said to himself.

Finally, he'd had enough.

'Wayan, I'm sorry, but you won't be able to stay here any longer because I have another guest coming tomorrow. You've been here for a week, so I guess you're ready to go home. You're probably missing your family and naturally they'll be missing you too. I understand and I won't keep you away from them any longer,' John said.

Wayan was surprised, but then he smiled and said, 'It's quite OK, John. I'm used to being away from home for a month or so. The family will be all right. Besides, my nephew hasn't seen Taman Mini and Ancol yet, and he also wants to look around for a job here.'

'But my visitor's arriving tomorrow and I'll be needing the spare room.'

'Oh, that's no problem. He can come. It's a big room. There's room for three. If necessary, my nephew and I can sleep on the floor.'

'But it's a family.'

Wayan was surprised. 'I thought you said the spare room was for one person. How come you've asked a family? How are you going to manage?'

'Actually, it's a friend of mine and his wife and child. But with you and your nephew, there'll be too many.'

'But I can stay in the living-room. I'm used to sleeping on a chair.'

'No, you might catch a cold if you do that.'

Wayan laughed.

'Oh no, I won't. I'm used to sleeping outdoors. It's no problem, John. Actually, I like a lot of people around. I could teach your friend's child to dance.'

John was perplexed. He felt he'd made his wishes known politely, but his guest didn't take the hint. He felt increasingly that his rights as host had been abused. Meanwhile, Wayan had turned his attention to asking his nephew to Taman Mini the next morning.

Finally, John came out in the open and threw them out.

'I'm sorry, Wayan, but you just can't stay here any longer. My visitors are arriving tomorrow. I hope you understand.'

Wayan was stunned.

'Are you telling me that I've got to go home?'

'That's up to you. The thing is that you have to move out of this house today because I've got to get it ready for my guests. You do realize that I'm going back home in a few days' time, don't you? A lot of my friends want to say goodbye to me and I have to give them the opportunity. Sorry, Wayan, but I hope you understand.'

Now Wayan's expression changed. He looked quite offended.

'But my nephew hasn't been to see Taman Mini yet.'

'I'm sorry.'

Wayan was thinking. He looked upset and flushed.

'Well, how about if I go home now, but my nephew stays on here for a few more days. He could sleep in the kitchen.'

'It can't be done, Wayan. Besides, I hardly know him. I invited you here, not him.'

'That's true, but he still wants to see the Ancol amusement park. What's the point of him coming to Jakarta if he doesn't get to see Ancol?'

John didn't answer. He was even more disgusted by the young man he considered to be an impudent parasite.

'You have to understand my position, Wayan. I'm leaving Indonesia shortly, and I want to say goodbye to all my friends. I'm sorry but I haven't got the time to arrange or think about anything else. Here you are, I've organized a ticket for the night bus. It leaves at seven o'clock. My servant will take you to the bus-stop. There's still plenty of time for you to get ready.'

John put a ticket for the night bus into Wayan's hand. Wayan was so surprised he couldn't speak. So, there was no ticket for his nephew, and no one was going to see him off. It was very different from his arrival—coming by plane and getting picked up by car.

Wayan was baffled. Why had the world turned 180 degrees? Why was his nephew being treated like this? He resented John so much. He was angry with this foreigner who had no regard for other people's feelings.

'You bastard! You're just like all whites! You always spoil everything,' said Wayan with a very long face.

He was forced to dip into his own wallet, which was actually full of money. He bought his nephew's ticket and they went home that night.

In the meantime, John was still waiting to see if Wayan would say goodbye at the last minute. But he didn't. He was too busy thinking about his nephew. Apparently, he was trying hard to get him to become his son-in-law, by marrying his daughter who was verging on being an old maid.

'You ugly devil, John. You're a typical white and you always will be. You want to be the boss and walk all over everybody and get your own way,' Wayan cursed as he sat in the bus. Beside him sat his nephew. He was wearing a new jacket, but had a disgruntled, sour look on his face. He was very disappointed at having to go back to Bali so soon.

Meanwhile, at his house, John was also complaining.

'My God, how could anyone behave like that! He's a typical native! A typical ex-colonial! He's still got the mentality of a slave!'

The Corpse

RAY RIZAL

'The Corpse' is taken from Ray Rizal's collection
Lukisan Terakhir [The Last Painting], published in
1990. The story is set in the world of the wealthy of
Jakarta. The author himself describes his story as a
manifestation of a sick society, which is symbolized by
a philandering husband and his mistress.

HE had become a corpse. That's right, just a few hours ago.
He died of a heart attack. That was the doctor's verdict,
despite the fact that till then the man had never suffered any
heart disease. The doctor's statement was probably the
simplest explanation for the death and was easy to accept.
He was saying that when a person stops breathing, the heart
stops working too. Some people consider that dying of a
heart attack is more prestigious than dying of asthma or
tuberculosis. And tuberculosis is a disease of the poor. It's a
different matter again with AIDS. People don't want their
families to be told they died of AIDS.

Anyway, the dead man's name was Birman. During his
lifetime, he worshipped ambition and prestige. Strangely,
there was no proud smile on his face when he had the heart
attack (if that's what did happen). His expression was very
tense and troubled. When he was well, he often used to
have his heart checked, just like most of his fellow wealthy
friends did. It was as though it was compulsory for busy

people who were president-directors to diligently have themselves checked out by heart specialists. Some of his friends apparently really did have bad hearts. They told everyone as though it was a status symbol. Birman was surprised and quite disbelieving when the doctor said his heart was healthy and not the least bit abnormal. So why was it that lately he often felt his heart racing?

Birman had a beautiful wife who was a very unpretentious woman. Her name was Cita. She spent her days looking after their four children, two boys and two girls. Cita actually had a degree in literature, but she and Birman agreed that after they got married she'd just be a housewife. Now she was nearly fifty. She was starting to get a few wrinkles, but she didn't have plastic surgery. Nor did she dye her hair which was going grey. She considered that those things were part of her maturity as a middle-aged woman. With a successful and loving husband and four children who were clever, hard-working and healthy, what more could she ask for? She had a house, a car, plenty of money, and everything she wanted.

*   *   *

'Come on, what are you waiting for? Hurry up and get dressed …,' Cita glanced at Birman. She'd almost finished dressing in her formal sarong and long-sleeved overblouse. Today, they were going to attend the graduation ceremony of their second son who had gained his economics degree.

'You go by yourself … I've got an important meeting this morning.'

Birman didn't stir from the bed, where he lay looking up at the ceiling.

Hearing this, Cita was startled, then walked quickly over to him.

'My God, what's this?' she said rather loudly, frowning. 'You've only been home one night from being out of town. How come you've got to have a meeting today? Dedi's going to be very disappointed.'

'He'll understand,' Birman said coolly.

Now Cita sat on the edge of the bed and looked closely at Birman.

'We've waited so long for this day. Why do you suddenly consider it's not important?'

Birman couldn't take Cita's scrutiny like that. He jumped up suddenly and strode off towards the bathroom. Cita sighed with relief. In front of the bathroom door, Birman stopped. He glanced at Cita and said firmly, 'I can't go. You go by yourself!' And he shut the door.

For a moment, Cita was stunned, and then she punched the mattress with her fist. She was furious. She almost made things worse by pulling out the elaborate bun in her hair. Fortunately, she quickly remembered how much trouble it had been to put it up. She took a deep breath. Before Dedi was told, she had to understand it herself first.

She'd always been able to forgive Birman, but particularly recently it seemed that the great store of forgiveness she provided wasn't enough. But she'd never lost patience. She knew him so well. They'd just celebrated their silver wedding anniversary. It was no joke when just after it Cita felt distant from Birman, but that strange feeling wouldn't go away, and Cita endured it secretly. When Cita had told him joyfully that Riva's parents were going to propose on their son's behalf to Heni, their first daughter, Birman's eyes had bulged. Heni and Riva had been going out together for two years.

'Do they think they can carry our daughter off just when they feel like it!' Birman said furiously.

Cita was astonished. She shouted a denial, 'They don't want to carry Heni away. She's still our daughter. She's just going to be their daughter-in-law.'

'But it's too quick, it's too soon,' Birman's voice was shrill and loud.

'What's too soon about it? Heni's finished her studies and she's a teacher. She's twenty-six years old. What else does she have to wait for?'

'The point is it's too soon, I tell you, it's too soon!' Birman had insisted.

*   *   *

Now Cita really didn't understand why Birman wasn't proud that his son was graduating, and why he wasn't happy because his daughter had received a proposal of marriage, despite the fact that that was what they'd always hoped for. Their children growing up, getting a degree, getting married, and having children. Themselves getting old and having sons and daughters-in-law and grandchildren. Being called grandmother and grandfather. So what did Birman mean by too soon? Getting old too soon, having in-laws too soon, having grandchildren too soon, or what? Cita didn't know. She herself didn't mind how soon she was called grandmother, because it was time for that, it was appropriate. If she was called grandmother, it wouldn't bother her at all. She'd fully enjoyed her youth, it was now left for her to experience old age. Age couldn't be bought. Everything had to be enjoyed, whatever it was. Money could be the means to complement happiness in old age within a peaceful family.

But Birman did use money to buy the youth of another woman. Her name was Sara. Her status was maybe that of lover, sweetheart, or mistress, but it wasn't that of wife. They were not officially married yet. A married man like

Birman could not just casually take another wife. At first, this wasn't a problem to Sara. She was happy to live with him provided she got money. She was tired of swaying along the catwalk as a model, with a meagre salary. With the money from Birman, she was free to buy whatever she wanted, free to take trips abroad, free to open a batik business. Of course, everything went on surreptitiously, behind Cita's back.

Being what you would call drunk with love, Sara accepted this situation at first. When you're setting a trap, you have to be patient. But becoming a wife is the desire of every woman even if it starts with stealing another woman's husband, and after she gave birth to a child, Sara demanded to be a legitimate wife, with a legitimate child.

'I won't go on being treated like this. I want you to marry me immediately.'

Birman panicked. 'But ... but I can't possibly marry you officially without Cita's permission. That's the law.'

'There's no way Cita will give permission, is there?' Sara attacked. 'That's why you'll have to choose between us. Her or me!'

That was the beginning of Birman's mental agony. Her or me ... her or me! The dilemma kept echoing with every breath he took. He trembled. His head felt as though it was cracked, his spirit cut in two. Meanwhile, Cita smelt out his affair with Sara. Now she knew the reason why Birman had become a stranger in his own household lately. It was true that he was frightened to have a son-in-law and a grandchild soon. No wonder, when he'd just had another child who wasn't yet three and a half months old. He'd be embarrassed, wouldn't he? It would be shameful.

Cita faltered. She was disappointed, angry, jealous, and hurt. For a month, she lost her grip. Her world was shaken as though hit by an earthquake. Her family and children held her close, giving her moral support so that she wouldn't fall. Until one day she was able to say coldly, 'Birman, you have to choose between us. Me or her. I'll give you one month. After that, if you haven't broken off your relationship with her, I'm going to the court to file for divorce.'

Birman was shaken. He felt even more terrified. Me or her ... me or her. Cita was saying what Sara had said. Cita was even threatening to ask for a divorce. Birman was very confused. He couldn't choose. He really couldn't. He wanted both of them. Sara had qualities Cita didn't have and vice versa. If he had them both, it would be perfect. But how could he? Two women of different importance, each having her own self-respect, aware of the law, and conscious of her rights. Birman was worried, not knowing which one he wanted to choose.

Up till now, he'd always got everything he wanted. Four cars, even four houses—no problem. But wives? If he had two, his life would be split into two. He reeled. There isn't a woman alive who wants to share with another, there isn't. They all struggle to get one man for themselves. Sara too was like that. She said, 'Just let Cita get a divorce. We can get married if you're divorced.'

Birman looked up in surprise. 'But I don't want to divorce her. Be patient Sara, I'll talk Cita into becoming a co-wife.'

Sara lost her temper. 'I know Cita doesn't want to be a co-wife and neither do I. I won't be a co-wife, do you hear? If you aren't sure, go back to Cita. Leave me, get out! Don't come back here until you're divorced. I'll expect your decision one month from today.'

Birman drifted around buffeted by the waves. The door of Cita's house was shut, and so was Sara's. Neither of the doors would open before he made a decision. But he really couldn't make one. He was too used to having both of them and frightened of losing one. Birman had trouble breathing; at the office, in the street, in the hotel where he was staying. He was squeezed between two currents. He let himself go. Sometimes he didn't eat and often didn't sleep. There was nothing left of the happiness he used to enjoy. His brain kept thinking to try to find a way out, thinking up strategies and tactics, but nothing could calm him. Suddenly, everything had turned to stone. If previously everything he touched had turned to money, now it turned to stone and the stones fell on him from all directions. Birman was pinned under them. He was crushed and couldn't breathe properly. And then his breathing stopped completely.

*   *   *

Now the corpse was lying stiffly in the hospital morgue. The body which not long ago had been warm was now cold and stiff. But no family had come to see the corpse, let alone look after it and take it home. It was still fully dressed in a grey safari suit, with watch, rings, briefcase, wallet, documents, and other things that had been found with it being held in safe keeping by one of the staff because he was frightened someone might steal them. They were all expensive items. Birman died in his car by the roadside. It was thought he'd had a heart attack when he was driving and had managed to park his car exactly in front of a 'no stopping' sign. The police lifted out his body which was slumped over the steering wheel and took it to the hospital. Clearly, there were no suspicious circumstances about the death. There were no signs of suicide or murder in the noisy broad daylight on the busy road. That was what the police concluded.

Based on the identity papers found on the body, the family was contacted. The police didn't use the telephone because they were frightened the family would get too much of a shock. A policeman and an official from the hospital came personally to see Cita. They were ready to face a wife who would weep and moan if not faint, which is what usually happened. But it was strange; this time they met a woman whose attitude was as cold as ice.

'Dead? Birman's dead? Why tell me?'

The man from the hospital was astonished. There were no signs of shock or sadness in the woman's eyes. Cita's tears had long since dried up, in the heat of extraordinary anger. They say even a banana tree will be scorched when it's touched by a woman in Cita's frame of mind.

'Aren't you his wife?' the policeman asked again.

'I used to be his wife but he hasn't been home here for a long time. Now I'm filing for divorce and I'm waiting for the court's verdict.'

'But now you're automatically a widow, because Mr Birman has died,' the man from the hospital plucked up the courage to say.

'That makes no difference. Even if he were to come home alive, I wouldn't be prepared to take him, let alone now as a corpse, which would just be a nuisance. Take it to his mistress, send the corpse there. Here's the address!'

The policeman and the hospital official left for Sara's house.

'Dead ... Birman's dead? What's that got to do with me? He hasn't been here for a long time. I've stopped expecting him and had enough of begging him to be responsible. Earlier, I asked him to marry me officially but he wouldn't divorce his wife. Anyway, he'd certainly want to go home to her place,' Sara spat out.

'But now he's dead,' the policeman interrupted.

'We can't ask him whose place he actually wants to go home to,' the man from the hospital added.

'Just because he's dead doesn't mean I want the bother of looking after things. Even if he came here alive, I wouldn't want to receive him. I'm sick of being made a fool of, being lied to, and being made endless promises. I never want to see his face again, alive or dead.'

The officials shook their heads. Because they didn't know the addresses of any other members of Birman's family, they were forced to report the news to his office. The whole staff was in an uproar. Birman dead? Cita and Sara refused his corpse? They immediately prepared the office boardroom, whispering like bees buzzing. There was no house of mourning for Birman, no house of mourning, no house of mourning ... the echo resounded in all directions.

The Puppet Bride

HASAN JUNUS

Hasan Junus was born in 1941 in Tanjung Pinang, Riau. He studied history and anthropology at Padjadjaran University in Bandung, West Java, and also studied at the Institute for Foreign Languages. In 1971 he returned to Riau and concentrated on writing and translating short stories and literary/cultural articles in local and national media. Since 1991 he has been resident in Pekanbaru, Riau, where he has worked on the editorial staff of a variety of media and also, more recently, as lecturer in the Faculty of Literature at Lancang Kuning University.

Hasan Junus's short stories have been published in *Horison* and he has also translated foreign literature into Indonesian, including the work of Sherwood Anderson, Jorge Louis Borges, and Herman Hesse. In 1988 one of his stories won a prize in the 'Golden Windmill' literary competition run by Radio Netherlands.

'The Puppet Bride' was published in *Horison* in 1991. It is an unusual story interlacing the life of an old woman with the fantasy of the puppet stories she performs.

THE Westerner, as the locals called him, started his day as usual with a swim at the beach. For three months, he'd been staying on that small island doing research on the twelve stories of the *cecak* puppet theatre. Bathed in the morning sunlight, he dived, swam, and hummed a song of his far-away homeland. No one took any notice of him any more. They were all used to him.

Suddenly, he cried out at the top of his voice and raced towards the shore. His shouts startled the women who were doing their washing at the well near the beach and the fishermen on the way home after fishing all night. His cry of panic was echoed here and there and people came running and gathered at the water's edge.

The Westerner waded in through the waist-deep water, carrying in his arms Grannie Lamah, the oldest woman in the village. Her long white hair hung loosely. The foreigner was mumbling unintelligibly to the people, although usually he was very fluent in the local language. Step by step, he neared the crowd that grew larger by the minute.

*   *   *

Where did it all begin? It began with a wedding. Not a real one. Only a game. A kind of play.

Stories all end with death. That's life!

*   *   *

As though standing in front of a phantasmagoric mirror maze, each episode in her life came and went quickly. Childhood, youth, becoming a wife, then a widow, all flashed past. Even her age, which was almost a century, didn't seem long to her. It may not have seemed long, but every incident was fixed in her memory like nail scratches on the surface of a mirror.

She was born on the small island which was formerly the centre of government of that island kingdom. Her father, who had suddenly become a widower when she was born, called her Salamah, which means 'she who brings peace'. But we all know a name is no guarantee of a person's fate.

Was fate kind to her because she married Encik Muhammad, an official in the high court of the kingdom? Whether it was or not, four months after they were married, her husband went to Mecca to deepen his knowledge of Koranic interpretation and Islamic law. He died there, far away in the country where he'd gone to seek knowledge.

Salamah couldn't remember exactly what year all that happened. She could only try to link it with some other incidents. She was married when....

But wait.

This story has to begin with another wedding. Not a real wedding. Just a game, a kind of play.

Since her brief girlhood, Salamah had been trained by her grandmother to make dolls from scraps of cloth about a hand's span in length. It was these dolls that played the parts in the traditional puppet theatre of that region which was called the *cecak* puppet theatre.

Grannie Anjung, the old woman who raised her strictly from the time she was small, handed the skill down, training her in everything from housework, good manners, and correct behaviour, to memorizing the dialogue of the puppet theatre stories, which had to be word perfect.

There were twelve of these stories. They all began with a wedding and ended with death. 'That's life!' Salamah would say, copying her grandmother's words every time she ended a story. She must have said those words thousands of times in her lifetime.

Her first official performance, after almost a year of practice, was held one night in the main room of her large house. The audience consisted of twenty women and children. Naturally, there was a ceremony before the performance.

Earlier, she'd been told by her grandmother to bathe and shampoo her hair because her first menstruation had ended that day. Salamah was dressed up like a child bride. Her clothes were fragrant from incense and pot-pourri of flowers made by skilled hands.

By the light of the candles in four five-branched cande-labra, Salamah performed her first puppet story, called 'The Dolphin Bride'.

Placing the cloth puppets one by one on the miniature stage of gleaming copper, the young girl, who had now reached puberty, spoke the prologue which she had been memorizing for so long.

'One day a female dolphin that was very pregnant lay in the shallows, careless because she was enchanted by the warmth of the morning sun. She forgot that the tide always goes out. At dusk, she was still thrashing around on the dry sand, struggling in vain, while the male dolphin swam round and round in the deep water, powerless to help his mate. Weak from exhaustion and pain, in the shallows, the female gave birth to a pair of young that with great difficulty crawled up on to the land and turned into humans. Night came and with it the bright moon to accompany them. Weeping, the dolphins swam back to their deep pool without their babies.

'Thousands of years later....'

The story began with a wedding, so it was a wedding that took place on the miniature copper stage. A stage that gleamed. The puppet bride sat on the bridal dais, and in front was the ceremonial glutinous rice, which was coloured yellow with turmeric, and decorated with eggs and coloured flowers made of beads.

Although the puppeteer could only move two puppets at a time, it was said that because of the magical atmosphere, the fragrance of incense and the mantras, the cloth puppets seemed to be alive.

Everyone was watching the performance in silence but when Salamah raised the level of excitement with the song of the wedding procession, it was as though the room thundered with the rattling of tambourines and the blowing of trumpets. The audience was mesmerized, as though witnessing a real wedding ceremony. They were watching a drama acted by tiny people but they felt that it was they who had shrunk to the size of the cloth puppets.

The large room was hushed with silence in the scene where the bridal couple fed each other a mouthful of the special rice. The bride's attendant took a little rice in her fingers, peeled an egg, placed them in the bride's hand, and raised that hand to the groom's mouth. Then she did the same for the groom and raised his hand to the bride's mouth. The audience cheered and clapped.

Then something terrifying happened. Suddenly, the groom collapsed, vomiting blood. The bride was shocked and leapt to her feet, screaming. A woman among the wedding guests stood up and said accusingly, 'The bride has poisoned her husband. Look at the long nail on her ring finger. That's where she hid the poison!'

With tears streaming down her face, the puppet bride left the room that was in uproar. She walked slowly, as though her feet were not touching the ground, and headed for the beach that was as dry as a bone, like an arid desert because the water had all dried up. Her soft, bare feet no longer felt the sharp pebbles. She walked straight to the water's edge and sat on a rock. The red sun faded and the purple shadows of the night began to appear. The pale moon made ready to replace the sun.

The bride undid the bun in her hair. Her long, loose hair stirred in the breeze. She kept the tide at bay with her tears. But nature became impatient and unwilling to be defeated by a woman's tears. They dried up and dry sobs remained which were more painful than the tears.

The tide which had begun to come in lapped the soles of her feet. 'The bride has poisoned her husband! Look at the

long nail of her ring finger where she hid the poison!' Water
started to brush her ankles. She looked at her long finger-nail,
bent forward, and stabbed the soles of her feet several times
with it. Blood mingled with the water around her feet. The
water came up to her knees, then her waist, then her chest.
She scratched her shoulder blades and armpits with the long
nail. The water was up to her neck. The sticky blood around
the rock where she was sitting mingled with the colour of the
night. The wounds on her feet, shoulder blades, and armpits
turned into scales and fins, the scales and fins of a dolphin.
Once again, she looked at the land and tried to weep but all
that remained were the dry sobs, more painful than all the
wounds. Then she swam off into the sea and the night.

At the wedding ceremony, there was panic. Suddenly, a
man rushed in and in a thundering voice said, 'Where is the
bride? I am her uncle. I had a premonition something
would happen tonight. As a precaution, I put some antidote
under my niece's finger-nail without her knowing. It was
medicine for her husband that was under her nail.' Then he
pointed to the woman who'd accused the bride, and
accused her of poisoning the groom with the help of the
bride's attendant. 'Where is the bride? Find her!'

It wasn't till then that everyone realized that the bride had
gone. A boy who had been standing near the door said, 'I saw
her sitting on a rock on the beach. When the sun set and the
tide came in, she swam away into the sea and the night.'

The twenty candles that lit the room had burnt right
down. Seven had gone out. The others would soon follow.
The dim light of those remaining seemed to be purposely
taking the story to its end. The cool light of the moon came
through the windows. There was no longer any smoke
from the incense, just its fragrance clung in the air.

The story was almost finished. The closing scene showed
the parents of the groom entering the room. The mother sat

and touched her son's head, stroking it lovingly and wiping her tears. The father sat beside his wife, holding his son's arm. He too brushed tears from his eyes. The bride's uncle went and sat by the door, and bowed his head, wiping his tears. And one by one the guests wiped their tears too.

With one touch of her little finger, Salamah released the catch of the screen at the front of the miniature stage. The screen came down and hid the stage. 'That's life!' she said, ending the story. Her first story.

*   *   *

Before Salamah ever had the chance to perform the twelfth story she got married. This time it wasn't the puppets which were in the festive bridal procession. It wasn't a game or a kind of play. It was a real wedding.

Then her husband went to Mecca. A month or so after that, Salamah was invited to the palace to perform the show in front of the Sultan's family. And that happened many times. But she was unable to finish the twelfth story which was called 'Biring Kuning's Rampage' because when she was performing it, she received news that Grannie Anjung had died. Before her tears were dry, the news also arrived from Mecca about the death of her husband. Then time seemed to fly. One morning, the small island was full of foreign soldiers. The Sultan left his centre of government. The beautiful island was looted and the buildings fell into ruin. All that remained was the mosque which the people looked after carefully. Kings and their high officials are fleeting creatures, only God is eternal. Time raced by.

One day, a young foreign man was introduced to Grannie Lamah, as Salamah was now called with the passing of time. He'd been living on the island for a few months. He knew every tiny detail about the *cecak* puppet theatre except the twelfth story. He tried in all sorts of ways to persuade Grannie Lamah to tell or maybe even perform the twelfth story. He tried flattery, money, and other people's influence. Finally, he used his trump card against the old woman whose memory was as fresh as a young girl's. He produced photos of Salamah's husband, and books of his writings, and his letters and notes about the puppet theatre. On the brink of despair, the young man was successful. She agreed.

Together with ten people from that lovely island, the foreigner had witnessed Grannie Lamah performing the twelfth story the previous evening.

Incense was burnt and the opening mantra was recited by the old woman in a trembling voice. But from where did she get the voice of a young woman when she began to chant the prologue:

Life is like dew on the leaves
Dew on the surface of leaves
Dew on the tips of leaves
And in that God-given dew
Let us bathe ourselves
And be cleansed.

When the groom's party came in procession to enter the grounds of the bride's home, his champion fighting cock, Biring Kuning, which never left his master's side, started crowing loudly, 'Biring Kuning is here … bringing the ceremonial betel from afar!'

But as they got closer to the dais where the bride was waiting, the cock seemed to become agitated and crowed more and more loudly. Concerned by this, the bridegroom faltered in his steps, but then continued moving towards the dais.

Because he felt he was being ignored, Biring Kuning suddenly struggled and broke free from the tie that was binding him. He flew furiously into the centre of the bridal area, and went horrifyingly berserk.

The cock seemed to become like a huge hawk. He swooped in all directions. Everyone lay face down on the ground, terrified. He wrought havoc with everything in sight. Curtains were ripped, the eggs and yellow rice were scattered and spilt on the body of the bride who had fainted. Only the groom, Biring Kuning's master, stood firm, but he was confused.

Exhausted by his rampage, the cock made obeisance to his master. The groom snapped angrily, 'Biring Kuning, why did you do this?'

'You did not understand my signals. I tried to tell you with signs but you still want words, things sharper than a blade, more piercing than a dagger. Well, here they are. This is an incestuous marriage! It cannot continue. Floods and earthquakes will strike, misfortune and disaster will be like clouds raining death upon us. The bride is your young sister! If you don't believe me, you can ask the old woman who lives at the end of the headland there.'

The groom picked up the bird and walked slowly away from the place. But when they had reached the gates, the bride's father called out, 'They have humiliated me! Go after them! Capture them!'

Thirty men dressed in black uniforms with krisses and spears in their hands appeared and chased after the bride-groom.

In the ensuing battle, with Biring Kuning's help, the groom killed the thirty men, but was himself stabbed thirty times, and mortally wounded. Biring Kuning too sustained many wounds and blood dribbled from his beak. Now his master lay beside the bodies of his attackers, not far from the end of the headland that was buffeted by the raging waves from huge seas.

Night fell. The bride regained consciousness. She left the bridal chamber and hurried to the beach. By the friendly moonlight, she searched for her husband.

Bodies lay strewn along the shore. The bride examined them, one by one. A woman approached her in the gloom of the night that was rent by the roar of the waves. It was the mother of the groom, the bride's stepmother. Together, the two women mourned over the body of the man they loved.

Suddenly, at the water's edge, a cock crow was heard. It was Biring Kuning. Although his wings were broken, he still managed to crow one more time before being dragged into the waves.

The screen in front of the miniature copper stage fell at the touch of Lamah's little finger. As though trembling in the wind, the old woman's voice was heard saying, 'That's life!'

*   *   *

It was late. The young foreigner and the guests who accompanied him earlier had all gone home. The snoring of the two women who lived with Grannie Lamah in the big house got louder and louder. The old woman was still sitting in front of the miniature copper platform which was the stage for her puppet play.

Then, one by one, she arranged the puppets at the front of the stage. The tambourine and the trumpet were heard, faintly at first, then louder as they got closer. All the puppets lined up in procession and headed for the side door that led to the sea. Biring Kuning crowed and was answered by the crows of a thousand cocks. Taking Lamah's hand, the Dolphin Bride opened the door that led to the sea and went down the steps and out into the peaceful night. In company with all the puppet brides in the twelve stories, Lamah danced upon the sea in the bright moonlight.

The Rosary

SENO GUMIRA AJIDARMA

Seno Gumira Ajidarma was born in Boston, USA, in 1958. He was raised in Yogyakarta where he studied directing at the Alam Theatre; then he moved to Jakarta where he studied film in the Department of Cinematography at the Jakarta Arts Institute. He has been a journalist since he was nineteen years old and currently works for the magazine *Jakarta Jakarta*. He has been writing poetry and fiction since 1975, and has had anthologies of poetry and short stories published.

'The Rosary' is taken from a collection of Seno's short stories entitled *Saksi Mata* [Eyewitness]. It presents a chilling picture of an incident that took place in an unnamed place in an unnamed cemetery.

'TELL me, Fernando,' the doctor said, looking at the results of the X-rays, 'how did these rosary beads get to be in your stomach for twenty months?'

The man called Fernando just sat with his head bowed and didn't reply. His large nose flared and his big eyes glanced sideways. His dark-skinned hand brushed his curly hair nervously.

'Tell me the truth, Fernando. I'm your doctor. How on earth can I cure you if you won't be frank with me about how your illness started? Tell me how these beads got to be in your stomach.'

Fernando still didn't look up. His mouth trembled. Every detail of what he'd gone through twenty months previously flashed vividly in his mind but his tongue still didn't move. His hands shook as he tried to control his emotions, his heart pounded, poisoned by anger, but great fear made him bow his head. He closed his eyes and saw darkness. He felt angry with himself because fear could torture him that way.

The young doctor who'd just graduated from university and perhaps felt he could only get a job in a remote area still persisted. He couldn't understand why a strong young man like Fernando found it so hard to speak, especially about his own illness.

'Did you swallow the beads because you thought they were pills that could make you better?'

Fernando looked at him from the corners of his eyes. He felt very sick in the stomach but the pain in his heart was worse, the pain of someone who'd been humiliated, insulted, and abused. He felt like telling the doctor to swallow his own stethoscope. His mouth opened....

'Come on, quickly, tell me. I've got other patients waiting!'

But the mouth had only opened, it didn't say anything. Fernando's thick lips opening like that made him look stupid.

'For God's sake, Fernando, speak! Say something!'

Fernando sniffed loudly and tried hard to speak. The doctor gestured with his hands as though trying to coax words from his mouth.

'A bayonet!' Fernando suddenly cried.

'What?'

'A bayonet!'

Then he passed out.

*   *   *

In the hospital, as he watched Fernando having an infusion, the young doctor tried to connect the word 'bayonet', which

Fernando had uttered, with the presence of the rosary beads in his stomach. He remembered when Fernando had first come to him. It was as though he'd materialized in his surgery out of the night and spoken like an actor in a drama.

'I'm ill, please help me. But I can't pay you.'

The young doctor, who was still single, hadn't actually come to that remote place to make money. He came because he wanted to avoid the corruption of the big city. He came because he wanted to treat people who visited him because they were really ill, not just because medical examinations were the fashion, as they were in big cities. So he didn't care about the words 'I can't pay you'. Yet the way Fernando said 'I'm ill' made him stop suddenly. In his eyes, the doctor saw deep pain.

'Help me,' Fernando had repeated. The tone of his voice really made the doctor understand for the first time what it would be like to be in need of help, and how it would feel if no one in the world would give it.

He looked at the X-rays of Fernando's stomach. The rosary was curled up like a sleeping snake. The doctor shook his head.

'A bayonet …,' he repeated Fernando's words. He knew what a bayonet was, a long blade attached to the end of a rifle. A soldier would use it in close combat, when he was out of bullets or didn't have time to shoot. The doctor often saw lines of soldiers racing about on training exercises, carrying bayonets. They often ran around the town, stripped to the waist and singing. Secretly, the doctor wondered why anyone would want to take on a job that could require him to sacrifice his life.

What connection was there between a bayonet and a rosary? Of course, there wasn't one. Fernando was the only one who could explain to him whether there was any connection between a bayonet and the rosary in his stomach, but he was now lying there unconscious with tubes in his nose and mouth. There was cold sweat on his brow, goodness knows what was in his brain.

In fact, pictures were flashing vividly in Fernando's head, pictures that no one could possibly forget even though he wanted to. Screams still rang in his ears, and he still saw people toppling like banana trees being felled. Then he saw the bullets and the blood and the terrified faces. Yet what always woke him up were the barked shouts, humiliating shouts that could only be uttered by men who felt that they had absolute power over the lives of those they barked at. Fernando was consumed by hatred when he remembered. He could never wipe it all away, but at the same time he was grateful because his hatred had given him the will-power to live.

It wasn't only soldiers who had the courage to die. Anyone had the courage to die to defend his life. Especially a life of freedom and self-respect.

'A bayonet,' Fernando whispered. The doctor moved closer. Fernando's eyes opened.

'A bayonet,' he repeated.

Then he passed out again.

The moon shone brightly above the hospital. If only moonlight could cure the sick, the doctor thought. He was very worried that Fernando wouldn't regain consciousness again. He would die with the rosary beads in his stomach and with the mystery which the doctor would never solve. He would never be able to fathom out the riddle of the word 'bayonet'.

When the X-ray was developed, at first he didn't know that those round objects were rosary beads. He thought they were peas. But of course peas would be dissolved and that would be the end of them. The objects in the stomach were definitely something insoluble. Maybe they were marbles. But they were too small for marbles, and, anyway, why would Fernando swallow marbles? They must be some sort of very hard seed, the doctor thought. In any case, if they were, why ever did Fernando swallow them? Finally, he asked Fernando.

'They're rosary beads, doctor.'

'When did you swallow them?'

'Almost twenty months ago.'

'Why did you swallow them?'

That's as far as the questions went. Fernando was never able to explain how the rosary beads got to be in his stomach.

If Fernando couldn't tell him, maybe there was someone else who could. But who was Fernando? The doctor remembered how he'd just appeared out of the night. In this town, it was very difficult to know anybody. They could appear and disappear just like that, into the night. Many people whom he'd met had suddenly disappeared and no one knew where they'd gone to.

Did Fernando have a family? Possibly. At least someone had given birth to him. But this wasn't a guarantee that anyone could answer the doctor's questions about the rosary. In that town, too many people had lost members of their family. There were a lot of people alone in the world and many also who'd completely vanished.

To this day the doctor could not understand how a town could be built on mystery. There were too many nameless graves, too many imprisonments without charges, too many kangaroo courts, too much blood flowing like water, blood from eyes that had been put out, from ears that had been cut off, from wounds inflicted by the blows of rifle butts.

Now he wanted to know whether Fernando had a family but he felt he would get a terrifying answer, such as:

'His father disappeared when their house was raided one night.'

'His older brother died in jail with his face battered to a bloody pulp.'

'His young brother fled into the jungle.'

'His mother was shot dead.'

The doctor went on thinking. Fernando was still in a coma.

*   *   *

The rosary in Fernando's stomach was still on his mind when the doctor walked home through the cemetery. He was doing this at the instigation of a dark-skinned nurse.

'Think about the rosary while you're there,' the nurse had said as she changed Fernando's tubes.

So now the doctor was walking through the cemetery. The moon was so bright that the wall, the bitumen path, and the leaves shone with a silvery light. For him, the nurse's words were very mysterious. He felt more and more that he didn't understand the town and felt increasingly foreign.

'Think about this rosary when you're in the cemetery, and think why Fernando spoke about a bayonet,' the nurse had said.

The doctor did try to think hard, because he wanted to know the answer. The rosary could actually be removed easily with an operation, but that wasn't what was bothering him. He was very anxious to know how Fernando could swallow rosary beads, tasteless things that weren't salty or sweet or bitter. He desperately wanted to know why Fernando had said the word 'bayonet' and why a nurse had urged him to go home through the cemetery.

Meanwhile, in his coma, Fernando returned to the past, when a soldier used a fixed bayonet smeared with blood to force him to swallow the rosary beads in the cemetery.

'I spit on your dream of independence,' the soldier had said, pressing his bayonet to Fernando's cheek. Around him, scattered bodies lay everywhere.

The doctor had actually totally forgotten that the incident had ever taken place.

Other Oxford Paperbacks for readers interested in South-East Asia, past and present

*Titles marked with an asterisk have restricted rights.